ALL BACKS WERE TURNED

Marek Hlasko

Translated by
Tomasz Mirkowicz

Introduction by
George Z. Gasyna

NEW VESSEL PRESS
NEW YORK

ALL BACKS WERE TURNED

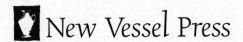 New Vessel Press

www.newvesselpress.com

First published in Polish in 1964 as *Wszyscy byli odwróceni*
Copyright © 2014 Andrzej Czyzewski
Translation Copyright © 2014 Julita Wroniak-Mirkowicz
Introduction Copyright © 2014 George Z. Gasyna

Library of Congress Cataloging-in-Publication Data
Hlasko, Marek
[Wszysci byli odwróceni. English]
All Backs Were Turned / Marek Hlasko; translation by Tomasz Mirkowicz.
p. cm.
ISBN 978-1-939931-12-2
Library of Congress Control Number: 2014936440
I. Poland —Fiction.

REBEL LIT SERIES

Rebel Lit is a new series by New Vessel Press showcasing works of literature that display a spirit of rebellion, challenge, heroism and courage.

The first in this series is *All Backs Were Turned*, by Marek Hlasko. The novel is a bleak and brutal look at the lives of a woebegone group of outcasts in pre-1967 Israel, by the Polish author known as the James Dean of Eastern Europe. Hlasko, with his startling good looks and his hard-boiled, existential prose, was an uncompromising artist who pointed out the hypocrisy and cruelties of society no matter the cost. Exiled from his native Poland, he drifted from country to country, using his pen to dismantle false veneers of civility and show the horror behind the masks he encountered. Hlasko wrote about a post-World War Two existence irreparably scarred by fascism and the Holocaust. Roman Polanski called Hlasko "a born rebel and troublemaker of immense charm." *The New York Times* wrote that he was a "spokesman for those who were angry and beat ... turbulent, temperamental, and tortured." We are proud to present *All Backs Were Turned* as the inaugural title in the Rebel Lit Series from New Vessel Press.

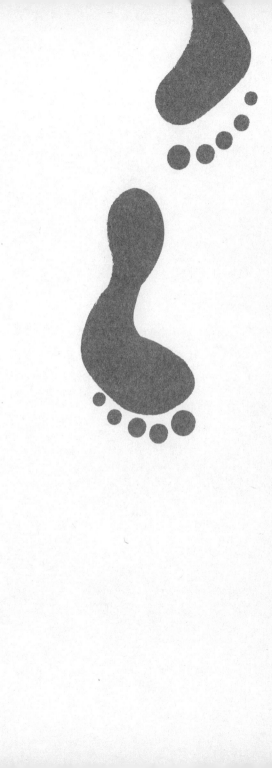

INTRODUCTION

THE INSCRIPTION ON THE GRAVE AT WARSAW'S OLD Powazki Cemetery reads, "His life was short, and all backs were turned." Indeed, Marek Hlasko passed away at an age at which many novelists are just coming into their own, entering what biographers like to refer to as the major phase. Hlasko was just 35—though years of eking out a marginal existence, frequently underemployed or resorting to what Poles of that generation called "black work," and a penchant for running afoul of the law, all conspired to make him look like he was in his fifties.

By most accounts (of those who knew and cared for him, at least), the final two or three years of Hlasko's life were a period of intense burnout, the tail end of a spectacular career that had launched him, at mere twenty, as the foremost voice of his generation—a deeply troubled generation, traumatized by the horrors of Nazi occupation, the Holocaust, and the violent Soviet-backed communist takeover of Poland that followed—and simultaneously its chief iconoclast. His earliest writings, set pieces of socialist realist psychodrama published in communist Poland while he was still a teen, are in the main forgettable, though even there, his fascination with the darker aspects of daily life, with betrayal, solitude, rage, and failure that would become his trademark is palpable; the unrelentingly grim, claustrophobic mood is only fleetingly punctured by requisite socialist platitudes, while the fiascos of the protagonists are final and irrevocable.

By other accounts, however, Hlasko in 1969, the year of his death, was about to enter a new stage in life. Having led a peripatetic existence throughout the previous decade, shuffling between various safe havens in Western Europe, Israel, and the United States—his native Poland declared Hlasko persona non grata in 1958, following the illicit publication of one of his novels by an émigré press, while he himself was in France on a state-funded fellowship—Hlasko was seriously considering settling down somewhere on the American West Coast, ideally the LA basin. When asked why there, of all places in the world, and in light of his halting English and a relative lack of contacts in the area, Polish or otherwise, his response was simple: "LA has good weather. I like good weather."

Was his sudden death on June 14 while staying at the home of his West German publisher, of an overdose of sleeping pills, a deliberate act, as the popular press insisted, the last spasm of stubborn contrariness on the part of socialist Poland's original bad boy, variously hailed as an Iron Curtain counterpoint to James Dean and as a communist Angry Young Man? Was it a consequence of ongoing disappointment and heartbreak? Or a merely banal though tragic miscalculation, exacerbated by immoderate alcohol use? We will probably never know with certainty. And perhaps it does not matter. Fellow author and adventurer Jerzy Kosinski, another of communist Poland's very bad boys and a fellow exile ultimately to the US—though his eventual suicide, in 1991, *was* by all accounts planned—possibly settled the matter when he declared that Hlasko "personally lived through what he wrote and died of an overdose of solitude and not enough love."

Hlasko began writing fiction while still in high school, and was publicly recognized early and often. He had movie star good looks, a roguish smile, and an ideologically "correct" past, having refashioned himself as an orphaned child of simple laborers, a housemaid and a fireman, when his father had in fact been a prominent attorney in interwar Poland. Hlasko said the right thing frequently enough when called upon and talked his way into the front offices of the premier state-run youth-oriented literary magazine, *Po prostu* ["The Way It Is"]. Surrounded by adoring acolytes of both sexes, guided by benefactors always on the lookout for the next hot new thing to use in the propaganda wars with the West, and even "managed" for a time by the then-chairman of the Polish Writers' Union, Hlasko was being groomed for his tenure as a shining star of Poland's new socialist culture. He was to be the poet of the transport truck and the proletarian suburb, a writer of youth and possibility—within Party-approved boundaries, of course. This was a role he initially assumed with enthusiasm, and it paid big dividends for a time, in the shape of fellowships, interviews, cash awards, vacations at writers' colonies on the state's dime, and the like.

In short, Hlasko's rise was meteoric; he became a legend in his own time, a paradoxical socialist brand. Yet on the elemental level of the myth, quite apart from the counterfeit past, a number of factors conspired from the outset to disrupt and undercut the facile image of the communist rogue with a heart of gold and a volume of Marx's *Capital* under his arm. For one thing, critics in Poland and elsewhere on the wrong side of the Iron Curtain generally referred to his texts as "behaviorism," a tendentious genre which encompasses thousands of volumes of novels and plays that appeared in the Soviet Union and Eastern Europe during the Stalinist era, and routinely featured "difficult" characters whose consciousness needed to be raised or modified. Few took proper heed of the black undercurrents of the work, or were willing to admit that Hlasko's true lineage was actually a fusion of the American noir thriller and Western European cinematic realism. Indeed, socialist realism merely provided a framework to be broken at the earliest convenience. Hlasko, then, was hardly the slightly disparaging painter of everyday life of Marxist utopias-in-progress, as many critics maintained (at least in their public discourse). Rather, in a true Conradian idiom he sought to "make you see," to partake in his own vision. And as the years passed, this vision diverged further and further away from the constraining dogmas of approved, formulaic "production novels"—novels that focused, literally, on "production" in farms and factories—towards dramas of power, lust, and revenge, dramas enacted between and among fallen men—men who are in turn elevated to the status of archetypes, symbols even.

In fact, the socialist heroes of even his early stories and novels, such as *The Eighth Day of the Week*, are no wise triumphant New Men with a flaw or two. Instead, they are broken subjects, unsteadily seeking their way within an inhuman system, sometimes improvising, frequently resorting to manipulations and lies as they seek to improve on impossible odds, their efforts more often than not rewarded with catastrophe. Already in 1956, at the peak of his Polish fame, Hlasko stated that his narratives, chock-full of brutality and heartbreak though they were, simply reflected reality as he knew it, that his protagonists were looking in vain for love and fulfillment in a city that never smiles. (Post-war, derelict Warsaw was the setting here, though any number of Polish cities and towns would have fit that bill.) Indeed it was socialist realism, that bastard genre of happy tomorrows pledged but never delivered on—since infiltrators, saboteurs, and eternal enemies lurked always and everywhere and had to be eliminated first—which presented the cynic's vision of life. The protagonist of *The Eighth Day of the Week*, an underemployed writer named Grzegorz, wrestles with the contradiction between what has been promised him of the brave new world and what has been borne out. In the end, he asks, "Can anything valuable come out of a world that has to use blackmail to keep from collapsing?" The indirect answer to his question, which he himself provides, is, "Waiter, half a liter, please."

From 1959 until his death, Hlasko led a life of exile: his petitions to return home to Poland were ignored or rejected by the regime in Warsaw, and so he roamed around Western Europe and Israel. Soon, what had begun as youthful wanderings began to resemble an existential imperative. By consensus, Hlasko's most intensely productive phase is the period between 1959-64, though even then, as an avowed "outsider," he shuffled between West Germany and Israel, sometimes for reasons practical—he was married to a popular German screen actress for a time, and had many acquaintances in Israel—but frequently due to factors having to do with the impossibility of finding true peace or a true home.

The texts either dating from or inspired by this chapter in his life, such as the short novel *Killing the Second Dog* (*Drugie zabicie psa*, available in English also from New Vessel Press), are unusually sparse, claustrophobic, oversaturated by color and light, and punctuated by images of surprising beauty which serve as a vivid counterpoint to the stark portrayals of brutality and humiliation endured by the down-and-out antiheroes. Combined with scathing irony, poignant vignettes of frailty, and an occasional wink to the reader, this semi-autobiographic world is a zone dominated by men, men who are often paired in their peregrinations so as to both complement and expose one another's weak sides. In fact, all the protagonists of Hlasko's oeuvre suffer from major handicaps; typically these are latent until foregrounded by inevitable conflict or are laid bare in dramatic outbursts of rare, abject honesty by the other, the companion, or by a woman who sometimes completes the triangle of interdependencies. This is a realm in which conflict is contested chiefly between men and, in an unhappily misogynistic turn, a realm in which the men are very frequently undone by (their inability to relate to) women. At the opening of the novel, co-protagonist Dov Ben Dov, a former Israeli Army officer who has fallen on hard times, is on trial yet again, this time for assault in a Tel Aviv club. When the presiding judge asks him for his name and demands that he answer whether he will plead guilty to the charges of "disrupting public order in the city of Tel Aviv on June fifth," Dov fires right back: "No. As far as I remember, there's never been any order in this city." Conflict is in the very bones of Hlasko's protagonists, and of his plots, and there are never any easy answers.

Expansive and self-congratulatory male bravado fills the entire canvas, but it becomes clear soon enough that the root cause of Dov's misfortunes, present and future—apart from his cantankerous, narcissistic father perhaps—is his spectacularly failed marriage. All the other men in the novel, whether friends, enemies, or mere bystanders, concur on this point. "She brought him down" is the laconic assessment of one of the peripheral men in the story, as he sits in a restaurant where he's just met with Dov. "She did," a passing waiter nods in fatalistic agreement.

As noted above, Hlasko's novels and shorter fiction, especially those produced in the late '50s and early '60s, including the work you have in your hands, are organized around two male protagonists who share the spotlight. However, readers have unequal access to their minds: one of them is typically given more attention, his internal world relatively more open to inspection, his motives less inaccessible. This figure is frequently construed in Hlasko criticism as a foil of the author himself, though any such overidentifications are risky. We often encounter the two principals while they are already on the road, in the midst of a longed-for escape from their problems, which sometimes involves their participating in some elaborate swindle or dealing with similar reversals of fortune fate has thrown their way. These two men are fellow travelers, and to some extent share a destiny, but Hlasko also posits them as rivals. Yet, while they despise significant elements of each other's personalities, they desperately need one another – much the same way as Beckett's characters in *Endgame* or *Waiting for Godot* depend on one another's presence even as they abhor it. This picaresque convention, the idea of setting out on the road with a companion, constitutes a time-honored literary paradigm in the Western canon. Hlasko borrows liberally from this convention, but further sharpens his encounters "between men" through the cinematic twist of extreme close-ups, abrupt perspectival changes, and the deployment of recurrent objects that may foreshadow dramatic action. In *All Backs Were Turned*, for instance, stones play such a symbolic function, evoking—among other images— Christ's parable on the doubtful virtue of guiltlessness and, more obliquely, the Genesis account of the contest between Cain and Abel. However, such scenarios of the friend/rival and the road do not appear in Hlasko's fiction merely for structural convenience or pedagogical payout; rather, they recur precisely because the protagonists keep stumbling into familiar situations, yet never seem to have learned anything from last time.

They engage in pithy sarcasm and constant one-up-manship—but the situation can also turn on a dime. The stakes are deadly serious, the categories of survival starkly elemental, leaving precious little room for maneuver. And justice, here on the frontier, ends up as a cruel handmaid of forces that our protagonists, preoccupied with scraping a living, with capturing happiness if only for a fleeting moment—and thus human, all too human, tragically human—are simply unable to grasp. Wrapped up in their fragile egos, preoccupied with their dramas, their backs turned, they never see that stone coming.

George Z. Gasyna
Associate Professor of Slavic Languages
and Literatures, University of Illinois

WEARING A BLACK HAT AND A BLACK COAT, HIS mournful face surrounded by a shaggy beard, he resembled a bird from some fantastic story; one of those fairy tales you tell children so they'll fall asleep, tales that belong to the horrors of childhood. He was sitting behind a table set up on the sidewalk in front of the courthouse; a typewriter stood before him. The man's clients were too poor to afford a real lawyer, yet he was no worse than any lawyer in this city. He knew how to write all sorts of complaints, petitions, and appeals, no matter whether the case had to do with alimony or a car accident, and he knew beforehand what the verdict would be. He could also supply witnesses of all kinds, ranging from innocent-eyed youths who just happened to be walking down the street when the accident occurred and saw everything that took place—or rather what, two months or even a year later, he told them they'd seen—to distinguished old men nobody would dare accuse of lying.

He adjusted his hat; rivulets of sweat were trickling down his neck, and the client fidgeted nervously. A clean sheet of paper had been inserted into the typewriter fifteen minutes ago, but so far the bird hadn't written a word.

"Does my case look bad?" the client asked.

"No," the blackbird said. "Everything is going to be fine."

"I thought so," the client said. "I want that man punished. I want him to go to jail."

"There'll be two trials," the bird said. "And he'll go to jail twice."

"Good, good," the client said.

"Not as good as you think."

"Why?'

1

"If you press charges against him, they'll lock him up. Then, as soon as he's released, they'll have to lock him up again. For assault and battery. You'll be the victim."

"I'm not afraid of him," the client said.

The bird didn't answer; he was watching a police van that had stopped in front of the courthouse. A young cop got out of the cab and opened the back door. Two men jumped out. They were handcuffed together.

"Take these off," one of them said to the cop.

"You have to enter the courtroom handcuffed," the cop said. "Rules are rules."

"We still have ten minutes," the man said. "You can handcuff us again later." Suddenly he turned around and saw the bird and his client; he started walking toward them, pulling the other man with him. The bird remained motionless when they loomed over his table. He watched the bigger man's bronzed, muscular hand shoot out in his direction and tear the empty sheet of paper out of his typewriter. The big man crumpled the sheet into a ball and tossed it away. Then he and the other prisoner entered the building; the cop followed, fanning his sweaty face with his cap.

"You were right," the client said to the blackbird. "I won't press charges. I'll save myself the trouble. There should be no quarrel between Jews."

"My feelings exactly," the bird said.

The client wanted to turn away, but the blackbird grabbed his coattail. "Hey, my money!"

"Money? What for?"

"Legal advice."

The cop led the two men into the courtroom, almost empty at this time of day. A man sitting by the window was inspecting his dirty fingernails; they seemed to interest him more than the handcuffs he was wearing.

"The judge is a good man," the cop said to the two men when they sat down. "You don't have to be afraid of him." He looked at them; the two men sat motionless, both suntanned, dark-haired, and slender, and when they didn't answer, he said again, "The judge is a good man. You don't have to be afraid of him. You'll know that as soon as you see him."

"They pay you for talking?" the man said. His face was swarthy, his eyebrows grown together, and he held his heavy head low like a tired railway porter or as if he were about to slug somebody. "Or just for being a pig?"

The man inspecting his nails jerked up his head, but the cop didn't say anything. A moment later the judge and the bailiff walked in and the man with the grubby nails stood up reluctantly.

"Are you going to testify?" the judge asked the cop.

"Yes."

"Are you ready to be sworn in?"

"Yes."

"Then take the Bible," the bailiff said, "and repeat after me..."

The cop placed his hand on the Bible. The bailiff stopped.

"What's this? Don't you know that you must either wear your cap or cover your head with your hand when you're taking the oath?"

"I'm sorry," the cop said, reddening. "I've come to Israel very recently."

After saying the oath he returned the Bible to the bailiff and signaled to the two men that they could sit down again. Then he sat down next to them and unlocked the handcuffs.

"Dov Ben Dov," the judge said, and the man with the joined eyebrows stood up.

"Date of birth?"

"January fourteenth, nineteen twenty-two."

"Place of birth?"

"Here," the man said.

3

"Marital status?"

The man didn't answer, only let his head fall even lower.

"I asked for your marital status," the judge said.

Again the man didn't answer. It was only when the man he had been handcuffed with—now sitting very straight in his chair like an eager student—touched his arm gently that he said, "Married."

"Criminal record?"

"You have all the information about me in that file," Dov Ben Dov said. "If you are to judge this case, you must have read it."

"Answer the question," the bailiff said.

"Yes," Dov said.

"Where is your lawyer?" the judge asked. "Don't you have a lawyer?"

"I don't need one," Dov said. "I have my own conscience; I don't need to hire anybody else's."

"You are charged with disrupting public order in the city of Tel Aviv on June fifth. Do you plead guilty?"

"No," Dov said. "As far as I remember, there's never been any order in this city."

"Defendant Dov Ben Dov will be fined ten pounds for contempt of court," the judge said, and then added, turning to the bailiff, "Make a note that if he doesn't have the money, he must spend three days in jail. And if he says something like that again, I'll have him thrown out of the courtroom." He turned back to Dov. "You can sit down now."

The cop nudged the other man forward. He was somewhat thinner than his friend and had a handsome, alert face. His shirt was creased but clean; he must have washed it in jail.

"Israel Berg," he said, not waiting for the judge's questions. "Born October seventh, nineteen twenty-five. In Poland. Single."

"Criminal record?" the judge asked.

"None," Israel Berg said.

"Do you plead guilty?" the judge asked.

"Yes, Your Honor, it was all my fault," Israel said. "Dov Ben Dov had no part in it. He was sitting quietly at a table when it happened. Actually, I am not even sure he was there. I was standing by myself at the bar when those men began to insult me."

"Have the injured parties come to the hearing?" the judge asked the cop.

"That wasn't possible, Your Honor," the cop said. "Those men were foreigners. Their sworn statements, however, should be in the case file. If I were you, Your Honor—"

"The court knows where the sworn statements should be, officer," the judge said. "Even if you find that surprising. Please answer questions and refrain from offering the court your advice. And remember to put your cap back on when you speak. Or, better, don't take it off at all." He gazed for a moment at the man standing in front of him. "Do you mean to tell me it was you who beat up those three men, that defendant Dov Ben Dov had nothing to do with it?"

"It all happened like I said, Your Honor," Israel said. "He's innocent."

"He sat at a table, drank beer, and watched you, a man lighter by forty pounds, take on three strong sailors, and he did nothing to help?"

"Everybody who sees us thinks that he is the strong one," Israel said. "But that's not true."

"I don't think you're telling me the truth," the judge said. "You're covering up for him because you know that defendant Dov Ben Dov has a whole string of such cases behind him. Such and worse. Manslaughter, brawling, and, before that, degradation, and dishonorable discharge from the army. And you know something else, too: defendant Dov Ben Dov is on parole. This means he has been released on condition that he keep his nose clean. This also means that if this court, today, finds him guilty as charged, Dov Ben Dov's parole will be revoked and he will be sent back to jail." The judge paused. "Nobody has been able to help him. What makes you think you can do more for this man than the army, his family, the courts?"

"I've told you the truth," Israel said. "I am aware I'm testifying in court."

"You're much weaker than he is," the judge said, "and yet you want to shield him. Even though you know very well that he started this brawl, just like all the brawls in the past."

"I am not weaker," the man said, and his face began to twitch nervously. "It just seems that way, Your Honor. I'm the guilty one."

"Defendant Dov Ben Dov," the judge said. "Stand up." He pushed his glasses to his forehead and peered from under them at Dov's dark, stubborn face. "Is it true that the man standing next to you is guilty? This man who is much weaker than you are? Answer me according to your conscience. You mentioned having a conscience, didn't you?"

"That's what he says," Dov said.

"And you sat at a table and drank beer, yes?"

"I don't remember what I was drinking," Dov said. "But when that fight broke out, my back was turned. I had dropped my cigarette on the floor, and I was looking for it when the fight by the bar broke out. I don't like leaving burning cigarette butts on the floor. That's what I told the police."

"You always have good witnesses, Ben Dov," the judge said. "Nobody ever admits he saw you brawling. This time it's the same. All backs were turned. But watch out; it may happen one day that everyone will turn his back when it is you who is getting hurt. Have you ever thought of that?

And what about your conscience, which you spoke of having just a few minutes ago? Does it allow you to put the blame on your weaker friend just because you know this is his first offense so he will incur only token punishment? Does it allow you to take advantage of a weaker man only because he happened to be there?"

"I told you, I'm not weaker than he is," Israel said. His lips had suddenly turned white.

"Are you sure?" the judge asked.

"Sure I'm sure," Israel said.

"Speak politely when addressing the court," the bailiff said in a wooden voice.

"I'm not weaker!" Israel yelled. "No, I'm not!" Suddenly he pushed the cop away, fell to his knees and grabbed the chair he had been sitting on by the leg; he tried to lift it up with one hand, but couldn't do it. The chair fell over and he, kneeling by it on the floor, began to cry in helpless rage.

THEY WERE SITTING IN A SMALL RESTAURANT BY THE sea; they had just finished eating. Israel turned to Dov.

"Do you think I can manage?" he asked.

"Sure you can," Dov said. "Many guys work there and they manage okay."

"You said before that maybe I wouldn't."

"No," Dov said wearily, "I didn't say that. You should know how it is with a new job. In the beginning it tires you out, then you get used to it, and then you stop enjoying it. It's almost always like that." He stopped a passing waiter. "Bring me a glass of brandy," he said.

"Don't drink brandy, Dov," Israel said. "Better have some coffee. It'll make you feel better."

"I don't want to feel better," Dov said. "I want a shot of brandy, that's what."

"Will he come?" Israel asked. "I'm beginning to worry."

"No need to," Dov said. "He'll come. Look at those girls and stop worrying." He pointed at two girls drinking coffee at the next table and held his hand in the air until one of them turned her head in his direction. "Just look at them."

"What do you want?" the girl asked.

"You can turn around again," Dov told her, letting his hand drop. "One more disappointment," he said, looking her straight in the eye.

A stout man in a khaki shirt walked into the restaurant. He stopped in the middle of the room and stood there, holding a pair of sunglasses in his hand. Sweat trickled down his face. Finally he saw the two men and began making his way toward them, never once apologizing to the guests he squeezed past, jostling their tables with his strong, heavy body. The chair he lowered himself into creaked loudly under his weight.

"Sorry you had to wait for me," he said. "It took me half an hour to find a parking space."

"It's okay," Israel said. "The important thing is that you came. We haven't been waiting long."

The stout man didn't look at him.

"When do you want to start work, Dov?" he asked.

"Tomorrow." Dov finished off his warm brandy and placed the glass gently on the table.

"Do you know what the pay is?" the stout man asked.

"No," Dov said. "But I know you. It can't be good."

"Whatever it is, it's fine with us," Israel said, but the stout man didn't look at him this time either. His gaze was fixed on Dov's face and the joined eyebrows.

"Dov," he said, "you had ten years to find yourself a good job and settle down. Why didn't you? Lots of people were ready to help you."

"When can we start?" Dov asked.

The man didn't say anything for a moment. Then he said, "You, Dov, can start tomorrow."

"That's not what I asked. When can the two of us start?"

"Dov, this is not a job for him. I never told you I'd have work for both of you. I said I'd have work for *you*. And only because it's *you*."

"You're wasting your time," Dov said. "We'll find something else. You have a garden by your house, don't you? So go home and water your flowers." When the stout man didn't answer, after a while Dov said again, "You're wasting your time sitting here."

"Why do you insist on towing him along, Dov? He's not your girlfriend. And he can't work at the jobs you can. You should know that."

"Yeah," Dov said. "Like I said, you're wasting your

time. Just get up and leave, okay? You haven't ordered anything, so there's no reason for you to stick around. They won't charge you just for sitting down."

"You're like a pretty girl, Dov," the other man said slowly. "Whenever two girls are inseparable friends, one is pretty and the other so ugly it makes your eyes hurt. You insist on taking this guy along wherever you go, even though you couldn't find a less likely man to team up with in the whole world."

"Gimme a chance," Israel said. "Believe me, I'm strong." He leaned toward the stout man. "Ask Dov. Yesterday we had a fight with some men in a bar. Ask him how I managed." He touched the stout man's shoulder, but the man shook off his hand and turned to Dov.

"Strong men always think they can do something for the weak. And wise men think they can improve the minds of fools. It never works. In the end strong men go down because of weaklings and wise men go mad because of fools. It's always been like that. How come you decided to ask me for help?"

"I'll tell you," Dov said. "I came to you because I was sure all honest and respectable men would turn me down. The way you did. And I know you well and know you're a scoundrel."

They looked at each other and suddenly the stout man burst out laughing.

"Hey, lover boy!" he shouted at the waiter. "Get us a bottle of brandy." He gave the waiter a shove with his heavy hand sending him halfway across the room. Then he turned to Dov. "Mark my words. There were once two wise guys in this world; one was named David and the other Goliath."

"Right," Dov said. "I'll remember that." He was looking straight ahead, at the sea, where the first lights were beginning to blink, then he turned his head to the left and looked toward the lights of Jaffa. "But it's better to be Go-

liath and die from a stone than to be David who became
king, but was the cause of many tears."

"You said that, Dov, I didn't," the stout man said. He
picked up a glass and held it in his hand. "You have a
brother in Eilat, don't you?"

"Yeah. Why?"

"When you were in court today, the judge must have
told you that if you got into any more trouble, they'd lock
you in the slammer for quite a while. Look, I know you;
you just can't keep your nose clean. Tel Aviv is bigger than
Eilat; if anything happens here again, the judge will forget
about your heroic past—"

"Skip that stuff," Dov said.

"Well, go to Eilat. That place is full of guys like you.
You can do whatever you like and nobody will bother you.
If you slug someone, the guy won't start yelling for the
cops, only slug you back. I'll give you my jeep; you can
pay me later. In Eilat you'll look up this guy I know working at the airport and he'll help you find tourists you can
drive out to the desert, show them around. Tourists like
taking pictures and bouncing their guts in jeeps; it makes
them feel like adventurers. And you'll be making enough
for a man to live on." He poured himself a shot of brandy. "Sorry. Enough for two men to live on. When winter
comes, you'll come back here and pay me my share."

"All right," Dov said, getting up. "I'll call our hotel
and find out what time we have to check out. I want to
leave tonight."

Women turned their heads to stare at him as he walked
across the room, but he didn't notice the looks they sent
him. He resembled a man walking across a cornfield and
parting the stalks with his hands.

"Funny, isn't it?" the stout man turned to Israel. "The
way a woman can hurt a man."

"Yeah," Israel said.

"When did he see her last?"

"A year ago," Israel said. "Maybe more."

"And he still thinks about her?"

"I guess so."

"She really got to him," the stout man said. "He's like a blind man now. Why did they split? Did he ever tell you?"

"No. He never talks about it. Not even to me."

"Tell him to stop thinking about her. There are plenty of other women around, thank God. Tell him I said that."

"Tell him yourself," Israel said. "Why wouldn't you give me a job?"

The stout man looked at Israel for the first time since he'd walked into the restaurant. He placed his glass on the table and said, "You should go away. You aren't suited for this country and you don't like it. Dov loves it. Too bad he'll come to such a stupid end." He gazed into the distance; his eyes were red and tired. "When I came to Israel, the man who worked in a kibbutz drying swamps, building roads, or planting orange groves was considered the number one hero. Now it's the rich American Jew who comes here to invest his money and won't even bother to learn ten words of Hebrew. So I, too, decided to start making money. Why not? I don't like to appear a fool. I'm telling you to go away. Take my advice, sonny boy."

"I'll get used to it," Israel said.

"Yeah, you might get used to this country. But you won't learn to like it."

Dov came back and sat down. It was dark now and a huge moon was hanging low over the sea, but the beach was still crowded and the heads of swimmers dotted the broad white waves far away from land.

"We might as well stay the night," Dov said. "They charge you anyway if you check out after six." He turned to the stout man. "Where's your jeep?"

"Outside. I came in it. I knew I had to give you this

last chance. Even though you'll let it slip through your hands, you dumb bastard." They watched his swarthy, meaty face and his thick fingers playing with the glass. "What does your dad do, Dov?"

"He lives with my brother."

"And how is he? Has he changed a lot?"

"He's eighty now. You don't change at that age." Dov rose, taking the jeep's registration card and the car keys from the stout man, but he didn't walk away yet. For a moment he stood there, not looking at the sitting man, and finally said, "Give me an advance. I need money for gas. I'll pay you when I come back for the winter."

"Don't you want my dentures too, Dov?" the stout man asked, but he reached into his pocket.

A while later he watched the two men cross the street and climb into the jeep, and for the first time he noticed how much they resembled each other. "This is how it had to be," he said aloud to himself. "That's why I came here. To give him my jeep and my money, knowing he'll waste it all."

"Will you pay the bill, sir?" the waiter asked.

The stout man turned to him. "Why do you bother to ask? Has the big guy who was here ever paid you?"

"There was a time when he settled his bills," the waiter said, adjusting his dirty cummerbund. He had a huge nose and a thin, tragic face. "She brought him down."

"Yes," the stout man said. "She did."

THEY ENTERED THE ROOM AND CLOSED THE DOOR. IT was difficult to breathe; even though they had walked a very short distance and climbed only one flight of stairs, they were both sweating profusely. Dov dropped his wet shirt to the stone floor. Outside somebody was singing in a high, shrill voice; whenever a bus roared past, the noise drowned out the song, but then it rose again.

"It'll be like this until morning," Israel said. He threw himself on one of the beds, first tossing the blanket covering it to the floor.

"Is that the beggar on the corner of Ben Yehuda Street?"

"Yes."

"The blind one?"

"Yes."

Somebody knocked on the door.

"Come in," Dov said.

A man slipped into the room; it was the desk clerk. He held a towel in his hand and every five seconds or so he'd wipe his face and arms with it.

"What do you want, Harry?" Dov asked.

"You left something in the shower yesterday, Dov," the man said. "Something you often use. Here, I brought them."

Dov turned slowly in his direction and took the two leather wrist straps the man held out to him; they were old and dark with sweat. He looked at them for a moment and then gave them back.

"I won't be needing them again," he said. "I've found myself an easy job."

"You didn't use them for work," the desk clerk said.

"I told you, I won't need them," Dov said. "You can

keep them or throw them away."

"No," Israel said, holding out his hand to the desk clerk. "Hand them over. I'll take them."

"But Dov said I could have them," the desk clerk said.

"Listen, Harry," Israel said, "the guy who was staying here before us left something behind. I'll give it to you if you give me the wrist straps." He reached under his pillow, pulled out a shirt and showed it to the desk clerk.

"Okay," the man said. He grabbed the shirt and gave Israel the leather straps. But he didn't leave yet. His gaze wandered around the room, and when he saw their canvas bag standing in the corner, he pointed to it and asked, "Is that all you have? The two of you?"

"Whenever I have to carry it, I wish we had even less," Dov said.

"We also have a jeep," Israel said. He pulled the clerk's towel out of his grasp and wiped his own face and shoulders with it before giving it back. "Now go away, we want to get some sleep. Hang that shirt in your closet together with all the other stuff you took from guests who couldn't pay their bills."

"I will," the desk clerk said, reluctantly moving toward the door. "So now you have a jeep and that bag. Good night."

"Good night, Harry," Dov said.

When the desk clerk left, Dov propped himself on his elbows and turned toward Israel. "Why did you give him your own shirt? What do you want the straps for?"

"They might come in handy."

"I don't want that to happen," Dov said. He watched Israel climb off his bed, untie the canvas bag, and put the two wrist straps, old and dark with sweat, inside. Then he looked at his wrists; two lighter rings showed where he used to fasten the straps. "My bones were always too weak. My muscles are too strong and my bones too weak."

He paused. "I once read a book about a man who had the same problem. Strong muscles and weak bones. I don't remember what book it was. I've forgotten all the books I ever read."

"Dov," Israel said. His face was tired now, but alert nonetheless. "Were you ever in Eilat?"

"Yeah, in nineteen forty-eight," Dov said. "When there was nothing there yet. Damn, what was the title of that book? It was the same as the name of the guy —"

"You think everything will go okay for us there?"

"We'll see. God, I wish that beggar would stop singing. I can't sleep. I keep staring at the floor tiles and I can't fall asleep."

He got up from his bed, took an empty beer bottle from the table, and threw it into the street. He heard the glass shatter; the voice broke off abruptly, but by the time he got back to his bed, the singing had started again.

"Dov," Israel said softly, "that man must be deaf as well as blind. There's nothing you can do if he wants to sing."

"I can't sleep," Dov said.

"Dov, why don't you make one more effort to patch things up with her? Maybe it'll work out this time."

"Does it ever work out?" Dov asked. He got up again and walked over to the window, his wide shoulders blocking it entirely. "What time is it?"

"One o'clock."

"We can leave in an hour. Try to get some sleep."

He took a green army towel and went out into the hall. Somebody was in the bathroom. He leaned against the warm wall to wait. A few moments later the door opened and a girl came out holding a pair of sandals in her hand.

"Oh, Dov," she said. "Remember me? I used to go to school with your brother—"

"Put your sandals on," he said.

"What do you mean?"

"Put them on. Don't walk barefoot around here."

"Are you crazy?"

He tore the sandals out of her grasp and threw them down on the floor. Then he twisted her arm.

"Put them on." He watched her slip her slim, tanned feet into the sandals, and then he knelt on the floor and fastened her sandal straps. "Now you won't catch cold," he said.

He entered the bathroom and locked the door behind him. He stood for some minutes under a torrent of cold water, then dried himself with his towel and came out. He saw a young man waiting by the wall; next to him stood the girl.

"It's him," the girl said.

Dov stopped in front of them in a circle of dim light. His face was empty, deadlike; now, when his eyes were shadowed, his joined eyebrows gave his face the appearance of a mask.

"Him? That's Dov Ben Dov," the young man said and turned away.

The girl caught his arm. "Coward! Stupid coward!" She pushed him away and came up to Dov. "If you're really going to Eilat, take me with you."

He didn't look at her face, which was very close to his; he was staring at her sandaled feet. "Give me your address," he said.

"Will you write me?"

"I'll tell you how it used to be in Eilat," he said. "There were no women there, and many of the guys were ex-cons who weren't allowed to leave the place. So five guys would chip in for a woman, buy her a round-trip ticket, and she would fly over for a day, sleep with all of them in turn, and leave on the evening plane. If things haven't changed, I'll write you." He stepped hard on her foot with his heavy shoe and saw her eyes turn opaque from pain. "If you want that, be sure to give me your address."

He shoved her aside and went back to the room. He closed the window, then opened it again and sat down on his bed, staring at his brown arms, already covered with fresh sweat. He wiped them with the towel, then wiped them again and threw the towel on the floor.

"Are you asleep?" he asked Israel.

"No."

"I can't sleep either. I think I'll never be able to sleep. It's all because of those tiles, Israel."

"You can't sleep because of the tiles? How come, Dov?"

"They remind me of her." He was lying motionless with his arms crossed behind his head, trying not to feel his own sweat and not to think about sweating. "They remind me of the first time I took her to a hotel in Jerusalem. It was so hot that when she walked around the room, she left wet footprints all over the tiles. As if she had just come out of a river. But it was all fine by me. I didn't care it was hot, I didn't care she was wet. Then she came back to bed and each time we made love we'd put a mark on the wall. And in the morning she said to me, You made one mark too many, Dov. No, I told her, I'm sure I got the number right. And she said, Dov, I love you. I don't want to argue with you over one little mark. She came up to the wall and wiped off all the marks. And she said, Let's start all over again." He fell silent.

"When did you last see her, Dov?" Israel asked.

"Eighteen months ago," Dov said. "The day we were supposed to get our divorce. But I met her the night before the hearing and she went home with me, and when I told the judge this, he dismissed the case."

"Why don't you go to her now, Dov? Tell her you want to try again."

"No, there's no point." He got up and walked over to Israel. "Can we trade beds? I want to lie with my face to the wall. I can't bear to look at those goddamn tiles."

"Go back to her, Dov," Israel said. He looked at the man standing by his bed, at his heavy, lowered head and the crookedly joined eyebrows. "Why don't you summon your courage one last time?"

"I've got something better than courage," Dov said, withdrawing his wallet from his back pants pocket. He pulled out a snapshot and held it out to Israel. "See this guy? He doesn't weigh more than a hundred thirty pounds. He's small, cowardly, and stupid. Look at him!"

Israel sat on the bed without moving.

"Come on, take it," Dov said. "Come on!"

"What for, Dov?" Israel asked, taking the snapshot. "Why do you carry a picture of your wife's lover with you?"

"To help my memory," Dov said. "There's nothing people fear more than losing their memory. And I fear it more than others. That's why. If I ever fall in love again, I'll take out this picture, take a look at it, and say to myself, Watch out, Dov. Every woman can leave you for a guy like this." He stretched out his hand. "Now give it back."

"No," the other said. "I won't give it back to you. We've been together for a year now, and all this time you've had this picture. No, Dov. I won't give it back to you."

"Hand it over, Israel."

"No," Israel said, getting up and backing away from Dov. "I won't give it to you, Dov." He tore the snapshot into pieces and tossed it out the window. "Go ahead and slug me if you have to. I get slugged from time to time. Why not get slugged once for doing something good?" He looked at the other's hands hanging helplessly alongside his body, then gently pushed him away, picked up the canvas bag from the floor and slung it over his shoulder. "Time to go, Dov."

"We can leave in another two hours," Dov said, sitting heavily on the bed. His hands were shaking. "We've got plenty of time."

"No," Israel said. "We're going now. We'll visit your wife. One last time."

The desk clerk came in.

"Guests are complaining that you two are so loud they can't sleep. Anybody who pays for his room has the right to catch a few winks, no?" He looked at Ben Dov's sweaty arms. "I can make you some tea if you want. Two teas will be half a pound."

"We're leaving right now, Harry," Israel said, turning to him.

"Stay here when you return. I'll give you a discount. You know I like you, Dov."

"No," Dov said. He got up from the bed and put on his shirt. "You don't like me and I don't like you. That's fair."

"You sure you don't want any tea? It'd do you good."

"No."

They walked down the dark stairs, got into the jeep and tossed the bag into the back seat. The beggar sitting on the corner of Ben Yehuda Street was still singing, even though the streets had been empty for the last two hours. Dov took out a pound note, crumpled it into a ball and threw it to the beggar. The man stopped singing and turned his empty eyes in his direction.

"You're a good man," he said. "And God will never forsake you."

"There are two of us," Dov said. "Why are you only talking to me?"

"You're a good man," the beggar said again. "And God will never forsake you."

"I told you he was deaf," Israel said.

"All right," Dov said, turning to him. "Then what are you waiting for? I told you which way we're going."

"Yeah." Israel let in the clutch. "The sun will be coming up in an hour. You'll see her then."

"You really think I should?"

"You have to."

"I haven't seen her in eighteen months," Dov said in a dreamy voice, resting his chin on his hands. "Eighteen months, Israel."

"It doesn't matter, Dov. What's important is that soon you're going to see her. Soon, at sunrise."

They left the city and were traveling along an empty highway. They could smell orange blossoms; the dark, hot, and heavy night air was alive with fragrance. The moon shone brightly in the middle of the sky and the jeep's shadow was as sharp as if it were day. A jackal crossed the road unhurriedly; they saw its big, luminous eyes. It wasn't afraid of the jeep and walked across the road with the soft tread of a tame cat.

"I wish she'd wear the same dress as the day I first saw her," Dov said. He was talking in a sleepy, tired voice, like a child telling its mother something before falling asleep. "A plain, light dress revealing her shoulders. I wonder how she'll be dressed. What do you think?"

"I don't know. Maybe she'll wear that dress. Why did she leave you, Dov?"

"I think it was my fault, Israel. I can never force myself to stop and think before I do something. I was probably too violent too many times; not that I act that way on purpose. I'm not my own creation, you know. It's not only others who have to put up with me; I have to put up with myself, too, and it really isn't something I enjoy." He paused. "Yes, I think it was all my fault. But I've learned something over these past months. And so has she, I bet."

It was five in the morning when they reached the village. They were driving past a row of one-story houses when Dov said, "Stop over there."

Israel parked the jeep by a long wall, three hundred, maybe three hundred and fifty yards long, over four feet high, which separated the village from the road.

"What the hell do they need this wall for? Do they run naked in the fields? Or are they putting together a vaudeville show and don't want any city rabbis to catch them at it?"

"No, that's where their garden is," Dov said. "Winds from the desert used to blow all the seeds away, so they had to put up this wall."

"Why are we waiting here, Dov?"

The big man pointed at a house standing at the end of the wall; its windows were still dark, the shutters closed. "That's where she lives. In that house. But she'll have to come out any moment now. She teaches kindergarten and has to walk this way to work."

"Why don't you go in and wake her up? Maybe that would be best."

Dov turned to him. "I'm afraid to. I know her."

"Don't be afraid," Israel said. "Remember what that beggar said when you threw him that pound note? 'You're a good man and God will never forsake you.'"

"That's her," Dov said.

The door of the house opened, and they saw the head of a woman who began walking very slowly along the wall. They saw only her head; the beautiful head of a dark-haired young woman, walking at an unnaturally slow gait on the other side of the wall. She walked as if very, very tired, the way old people walk; then she stopped and tied a white kerchief around her head. She started moving again; they couldn't see her legs or her body, only her head moving along the top of the green wall, then the wall ended, and they saw that the woman was five, maybe six months pregnant.

When at six in the afternoon they reached Eilat, a crusty layer of reddish dust covered their shirts and faces. They drove to the airport and stopped by the barracks housing the head office; Dov went inside, while Israel waited in the jeep. He looked at the mountain range, red in the setting sun; then he turned his head toward the bay. The sea was smooth and dark, and the beach was filling with people gathering there after work. A Dakota plane rose heavily from the ground; it made a half circle over the bay, then started climbing higher and higher to fly over the mountains. Dov came out of the barracks.

"We have to wait. Little Dov will be here soon."

"Who?"

"Little Dov, my brother."

Dov stood by the jeep, scraping the red crust off his face and arms.

"Your brother was named the same name as you?" Israel asked. "But that's a deadly sin!"

"My father's the one to blame," Dov said. "You don't know our Pop. When my brother was born, my mother had already decided on a name for him, but Pop was mad at her over something. He hated her all his life. My name will be good enough for him, he said. My father gave it to me and I'm glad he did. The kid will be glad too. And then he called me over and asked, Do you like your name, Dov? I said I did, so he turned to my mother and said, See? This one is satisfied; the other one will be too. Everybody cried and begged him to reconsider, but he was stubborn as a mule. And so my brother was named Dov just like me. After that the rabbi wouldn't speak to my father."

"And how do you call your brother?"

"Little Dov."

A truck pulled up a few yards away from them and a young man riding on its step jumped off. He was blond and tall; walking in their direction he held his head low in the same way as Dov, who was standing by the jeep with his shirt, soaked with sweat, in his hand.

"Hi," Dov said. "How's the old man?"

"Same as ever," Little Dov said. "Have you forgotten?

23

In a couple of days you'll be cursing the sight of him." He turned to Israel, looking him over without a smile. "This your friend, Dov?"

"Mine and yours," Dov said. "Let's go. I'm hungry, but I have to stop by a garage first."

"Something wrong with your jeep?"

"I want them to change the oil and give me a new filter. The oil looks like tar, and the filter must be clogged with this goddamn dust."

They stopped by a small garage. The owner had just changed into his street clothes; he got angry when he heard what Dov wanted.

"You want me to do it now?" he asked. "Isn't it enough that I get up at four? I'll sell you the oil and filter, but you'll have to change it yourself. You can use my grease pit."

"Where is it?"

"Over there." He directed them to the pit. It was short and narrow; the walls along its sides were so close together the men had to climb over the back to get out of the jeep. Dov lowered himself into the pit; it was barely three feet deep. He hit his head against the bumper while removing the oil-pan plug with a spanner.

"Fucking hole," Dov said.

"Don't blame me, I'm not the one who's running this country," the owner said, tossing him two one-gallon cans of oil and a filter. He didn't go away, only stood there regarding the three men with a hopeless, disappointed stare. "I dug it out myself. I had two inspections from the town council and each time they told me I had to make it deeper." Suddenly he gave them a happy smile. "Quite a few guys have busted their heads in my pit."

"So will you one day," Dov said. "And your wife will be free at last to marry your partner. They've been planning it for years." He backed the jeep out. "Hop in," he said to Israel and his brother. "Do we eat at home or should I stop by a restaurant?"

"Let's go straight home," Little Dov said, getting in.

They drove slowly, raising a cloud of reddish dust. The sun was climbing over the mountains, which didn't look so red anymore; they were dark and distant.

"Now turn left and stop," Little Dov said, and when Dov parked the jeep in front of a small house, he added, "and try not to provoke the old bastard."

"That won't be easy," Dov said. He took the canvas bag from the back seat and slung it over his shoulder. "One day he's going to bite his own hand and die of rabies."

They went inside. Little Dov opened the door to one room and let them through. An old man sitting at the table lifted his eyes.

"Look, Pop, look who's here," Little Dov said. "And he seems to be in top form, too."

"Where is Dina?" the old man asked.

"I don't know, Pop," Dov said.

"You come to me, your old father, and you can't tell me where your wife is?"

"She's a bad woman, Pop," Dov said. He spoke with an effort, his eyes fixed on the old man who had begun to tremble with anger. "Forget her."

"Women aren't good or bad," the old man said. "But some men just don't know how to handle them. I spent thirty years with your mother, and for thirty years she did what I told her. And thought what I thought. Where is Dina, your wife?"

"She's with another man," Dov said. "She's going to have his bastard."

"You come to me, your old father, and tell me you married a whore? Is that why I fled to this land to father you, so you'd be born free? Is that why I swore to God that I'd give my children freedom, and paid for it with my health and years of hard labor?" He threw Dov a wild, maniacal look. "Where is Dina, Dov?" he yelled.

Dov picked up a glass of water from the table and took a sip. His teeth clinked against the glass.

"You're old, sick, and mad," he said to his father. "That's all I have to say to you. You're cruel like a child. But you're old, and soon you'll die."

"Have you finished drinking?" the old man asked.

"Yes."

"Then put the glass back on the table."

When Dov did, the old man picked it up and threw it against the wall with all his strength. The three men leaped aside.

"And so it will be with anything you touch in my room," the old man said. "Don't ever come in here again until you go back to Dina or she comes back to you. You're not a man, Dov. Now go away, all of you, and close the door."

They walked out of the room and filed into the kitchen. Little Dov took three beers out of the refrigerator and placed them on the table.

"What a charming man our Pop is!" he said. "Too bad he's a Jew. If he wasn't, he could play the tooth fairy in plays for little kids." He turned to Israel. "How do you find the old bastard?"

"I feel sorry for him," Israel said.

"I don't," said Little Dov. "My wife often cries because of him."

The door opened and a young woman entered the kitchen.

"My wife, Esther," Little Dov said. "And this is my brother, Dov."

"I've been hearing all kinds of stories about you," Esther said, stopping in front of Dov. "But I'm glad you're here." She held out her hand and he took it gently, surprised how slim and fragile it was. "I'm glad you're going to help us."

"How can I help you, Esther?" Dov asked. He was sitting tiredly on a chair; he had pulled off his shirt, and they could all see his hard bronzed shoulders.

"It's got to do with my fishing, Dov," his brother said.

"You're the fisherman, not me. I hate fish. I'm sorry, but I never liked them. I do like herring, but only when I'm drinking vodka. And you don't drink. Don't ever start. You'll save yourself lots of trouble."

"Dov," his brother said, "do you know how much I made this year? Two thousand eight hundred pounds. And the season is almost over. I don't think I'll make four thousand this year. You know how much I made last year? Eleven thousand."

"I told you I'm not a fisherman," he said. "I can try lending you a hand, but I don't think I'll be of much use."

Little Dov walked to the window and pulled the curtain aside. "Come here, Dov," he said to his brother.

Dov stepped up to him, a bottle of beer in his hand; he leaned against the wall and then quickly drew away from it. They all saw the dark stain on the wall where he'd touched it with his bare back.

"I don't need to admire the view," he said. "I know Eilat. I was here in nineteen forty-eight, when we took the place." He took a swig of beer from his bottle and placed it on the table. "Our whole force consisted of fourteen army jeeps."

"Look at that truck, Dov."

"It's an old GMC. We had them in the army."

"It belongs to some guys who fish here, Dov," his brother said. "They're stealing my fish and my money. They didn't come to Eilat of their own free will, like I did. They were sent here by the police. For them, fishing is a nice cozy job. They've got motorboats; they can catch as many fish as they want. My fish. And now they bought this truck and make more money than they ever dreamed of in jail."

"The sea belongs to everybody," Dov said. "It can't be fenced off with barbed wire. I'm sorry. I can't help you."

"Those guys know you."

"But I don't want to know them."

"They know you, and they fear you."

"That's silly," Dov said. "They shouldn't be afraid of me. I mean them no harm."

"I thought—"

"I know what you thought," Dov said. "You thought that when your big brother came, he'd beat them up for you. Nothing doing. I'm almost forty. I want peace and quiet. And one more thing: if I start even the tiniest brawl, they'll put me behind bars for a few years. Remember, I'm on parole. If anything happens, I go right back in the slammer. If I jostle somebody in the street, it's all they need to lock me up." He took the bottle of beer his brother was holding in his hand and finished it with one gulp. "Look, if my presence in this house bothers you in any way, just tell me. I'll move to a hotel."

"No," Little Dov said. "You're my brother." He paused. "You really won't help me, Dov?"

Dov raised his tired eyes.

"See that bag in the corner?" he asked. "Do you see it?"

"Yes," Little Dov said.

"That's all I have. The jeep isn't mine. Try to live differently than I did." He slowly stepped up to Esther and pulled her into the center of the kitchen, into the circle of light. "You have a beautiful wife." He placed his heavy hands on her shoulders. "You don't want to lose her. Try to live differently than I did, that's all I can say."

"I heard those guys want to buy another boat," Little Dov said. "If they do I might as well pack my bags and leave Eilat."

"So leave. You're young and you have a beautiful wife.

All you need to be happy is a bed and neighbors who sleep hard." He went to the corner and picked up his bag. "Where will we sleep?"

"I thought I'd put you up in Pop's room," Little Dov said. "But now I guess you'd better sleep with us."

"In the same room with you and Esther?"

"You're my brother."

"Yes, I'm your old, worthless brother who is unable to help you. I'd like to get some sleep now. We didn't sleep at all last night."

"Fine."

They went into the bedroom. Israel pulled out two blankets from their bag; Esther gave him two more.

"These will be enough," Dov said. "Here, in Eilat, almost everybody sleeps on the floor. Are you two going to bed, too?"

"No," Little Dov said. "I'd like to borrow your jeep and take Esther to the beach." He paused. "I don't have a car." He walked over to the window and closed it. "Can't they park that goddamn truck somewhere else?" He paused again. "Can I borrow the jeep?"

Dov gave him the keys and said, "Good night. Good night, Esther."

She didn't say anything. For a moment she stood in the doorway, then turned and left. Soon afterward Dov and Israel heard the roar of the jeep's engine. They turned off the light, but neither of them could fall asleep at once.

"Tiles again," Dov said. "Last night I was looking at them, now I have to lie on them."

"Think about something else."

"Too bad we don't have any sleeping pills. I won't be able to sleep. When Dina was with me, I never needed any pills." He propped himself on his elbows. "You know, sometimes I would drop off to sleep on top of her, and she'd lie like that half the night, not moving so as not to wake me."

Israel didn't say anything. They lay in the dark listening to their own breathing. Through the wall they could hear the monotonous voice of Dov's father, praying.

"He's such a contrary bastard he even says his prayers at night and not in the morning," Dov said. "He does everything he can to make people hate him. And he quarrels with everybody, even God." He pounded the wall with his fist. "Let us sleep! Maybe you don't need your rest, but others do!"

They heard the old man's steps coming down the hall. Dov jumped up, picked up a chair from the floor, and lifted it over his head. Israel threw himself against him. The old man entered the room and pointed at Dov with his hand entwined up to the shoulder with a leather strap from his phylacteries.

"I would listen to you, son," he said in his shrill, old man's voice, "if you were a man. But you're not. I don't know what it is you lack, but you must be lacking something if your wife has left you. If you want something from me or your brother while you're in this house, ask. Never tell us what to do."

He left, closing the door softly.

LITTLE DOV DROVE SLOWLY; IT WAS DARK NOW AL-
though the moon was still out, suspended over the
mountain range—the desert lay shrouded in darkness and
quiet, without light, without sound, and yet they could
still smell it, smell the invisible waves of heat it sent out
tirelessly. He drove toward the beach, swerving to the
right a little awkwardly and too sharply whenever a car
came from the opposite direction.

"Do you want to swim, Dov?" Esther asked.

He turned to her; it seemed to him that he could see
her profile in the dark—the high forehead, the short,
straight nose, the strong neck. "No, I don't," he said. "I
didn't say anything about swimming."

"Dov," she said, "we did it twice already today. Please,
Dov, no more."

The right-hand wheels rasped against the sand as he
pulled her to him. "Did we really? I have a bad memory,
Esther. Like all men who work too hard."

"Please, I just can't," she said.

"You won't know that for sure until you try."

Near the airport he turned left off the highway. They
began bouncing up and down as the jeep made its way
over the rough terrain. Esther caught his arm.

"No, Esther," he said. "Put your hands around my
neck and hug me."

"Yes," she said. She did what he asked, but even in the
darkness she felt embarrassed.

Little Dov stopped being aware of the smell of the sea:
he inhaled only the smell of her skin, gentle and strong
like the scent of fresh bread. He felt her breath on his
neck, hot and clean like a child's. Unable to go on driving,
he stopped the jeep, jumped out, and held out his hand

31

to her. "Come."

"There are people here, Dov."

"Don't be ashamed, Esther. You're pretty and clean, and you smell like fresh bread."

He knelt on the sand and so did she, then he lay down next to her and started peeling off her dress and her swimsuit.

"You're like an animal, Dov," she said. "It's really a miracle that you can speak and read. And that you have a kind heart. Yes, you're an animal."

"And you're my wife, Esther, and I love you," he said. "Do you think many men love their wives? Think about it, Esther."

He could feel her hands pushing his belly away; weak, hot hands that couldn't put up much resistance.

"Dov," she said. "Dov, I hurt all over inside. If you really love me—"

"Don't worry. When you get hot and moist, it won't hurt."

"But I'll scream, Dov. You know I always scream. I can't control myself."

He got up, unsteady on his legs, and went to the jeep. He pulled the starter and the engine roared into life.

"Now you can scream all you want, Esther. All you want."

He felt her hands tighten on his back, and then a great joy began to mount in him, he was getting closer and closer to something he could never reach and where he could never stay, and then his head was empty of all thought and he heard the sound of his own teeth grinding sand. He lay exhausted, feeling her hands on his face, brushing it clean.

"Esther," he said after a while, looking at her face, now pale and tired. "You know how to make me happy. And you always will."

Suddenly he heard footsteps. He got up and lit a cigarette, feeling the weight and awkwardness of his own hand.

"Dov?" someone said in the dark. "Anything wrong? You need help?"

"No, I don't need help, damn you."

"Then why is your engine running?"

"That's what it's for. I didn't invent it. Now leave me alone, okay?"

The man went away. Little Dov sat down next to Esther; she gazed up at him and watched his crooked mouth inhale the smoke.

"Why is your mouth always crooked, Dov?"

"When I was a kid, I fell and busted my septum. A surgeon could have fixed it, but my father wouldn't hear of it. I had to twist my mouth to breathe normally. My nose healed with time, but this leer remained." He tossed the cigarette butt away and lay down beside her; the sand was as hot as during the day. He started to move his hands over her body and again felt his jaws begin to clench.

"No, darling," she said. "I can't. I'm hurting all over inside."

"Esther," he said quietly, "go into the sea and swim around a bit. And then come back to me. I can't throw my brother out. And I don't want to make love to you with him there." He reached for her swimsuit and helped her put it on. "Now go for a swim."

"Dov," Esther said.

"Yes, baby?"

"I don't know if I should tell you this, but I'm afraid."

"Of what, Esther?"

"Your brother."

"Don't be afraid of him," he said. "He's not a bad man. He's unhappy, that's all."

"People have been saying so many bad things about him."

"That's not his fault. People often can't tell the difference between badness and misfortune. Though I don't blame them for it."

He turned off the jeep's engine and they started walking toward the sea, passing through hard, invisible walls of heat the day had left behind. Then Little Dov sat down in his boat, which he always beached in this spot, and watched Esther swim quickly out of sight; she was a good, fast swimmer—young, long-armed, and long-legged.

"Enjoying yourself with the little woman, Dov?" suddenly somebody asked.

Little Dov turned around; there was a man in the motorboat beached alongside his boat and propped on two stays; the man was hammering something.

"Are you trying to insult me?" Little Dov asked.

"God forbid!" the man said. "It's enough that you feel insulted just because we fish in the same bay."

"You don't know how to fish," Little Dov said. "You try, but what of it? If you didn't have a motorboat, you'd never catch anything."

"You too will have a motorboat one day," the other said soothingly. "Come here and have a drink with me."

"Okay," Little Dov said. He jumped out of his boat and went over. Accepting the bottle and the mug the man handed to him, he poured himself a drink, tossed it down, then placed the bottle on the boat's wooden rail. "What are you doing here?" he asked.

"I couldn't sleep in the house," the man said. "I don't have air-conditioning yet and it's suffocating inside. So I thought to myself, why not take a blanket and try sleeping in the boat? But I get bored when there's nothing to do, so I started spiking these shoes." He heaved into sight the one he was holding—a heavy army shoe with spikes in it. "This boat rocks terribly, Dov, whenever I take it away from shore. Maybe if I drive spikes into the soles I can stand better on my feet."

"If you had a normal boat, it wouldn't rock so hard," Little Dov said, pouring himself another drink.

"You're right. But then I wouldn't be making as much as I do. Look at these shoes; nobody gave them to me. I had to earn the money and then go and buy them. And I had to pay twelve pounds for them here in Eilat, even though in Jerusalem or Haifa the same kind of shoes cost only seven or eight. I didn't come to Eilat because I wanted to, Dov."

"Lemme see the shoe," Little Dov said.

He took the shoe and weighed it in his hands for a few seconds before giving it back. "It looks like a shark's mouth," he said. "The problem is that none of you guys came here of your own free will. The police sent you here, and I know why. Everyone knows why. You, Yehuda, were caught stealing. Your friend Moses was banished for smuggling and for killing two Arabs on a street in Jerusalem five years ago. Supposedly in self-defense. As for that bastard who's your third partner, God only knows what he did, but he sure deserved a cooler place than Eilat."

"God's not the only one who knows," Yehuda said. "He himself also knows why he got sent here; he butchered a certain bloke who got in the way of his business. He's very strong, Dov. Problem is, he doesn't know his own strength. I worry about him sometimes."

Little Dov saw Esther come out of the water and start walking slowly in their direction across the stretch of white sand.

"I'll be off now," he said to the man. "Thanks for the drink."

"Hey, Dov!" Yehuda said. "One more thing. Don't play too much bouncy-bouncy with the little woman. Conserve your energy; you'll need it tomorrow for rowing your boat."

"Don't worry about me," Little Dov said. "I've got energy to spare!" Suddenly he spun around, grabbed the man by the neck, and dragged him out of the boat. He hit him twice in the face with his fist, and when the man fell to the ground, he kicked him in the head. "This has nothing to do with your fishing here or your motorboats," he said. "You insulted my wife."

Yehuda rose slowly to his feet. He touched his head with his hands and then looked at them: they were wet with blood. "Dov Ben Dov," he said under his breath, "you don't even know, boy, how much I pity you."

"Your shoe," Little Dov said, kicking with fury the shoe lying in the sand. "So you can stand on your feet, you fucking thief! Come, Esther!"

They got into the jeep and drove back to the dark highway leading to the airport.

"Just like your brother," Esther said. "He can't control himself either." She moved closer to him. "I don't want to lose you, Dov. Promise me you won't fight with any of those men again."

He didn't answer her; he drove in silence, his hands clenched on the steering wheel, and it was then that she first noticed how strongly he and his brother resembled each other in everything they did; the way they talked, the way they moved ... But she was too tired to think it through; she fell asleep with her head on his shoulder and didn't wake up even when he gathered her in his arms and carried her inside. After placing her on the bed, he turned around and gazed at his brother and Israel sleeping in one corner; he listened for a while to their heavy, tired breathing, then he undressed Esther and covered her with a sheet. But the hot body lying alongside his own prevented him from falling asleep; after three wakeful hours, when the night was nearing its close, he covered Esther's mouth with his hand and took her quickly and in silence. Afterward he drew the sheet, wet and heavy with his sweat, over his own body.

"Esther, don't be angry at me for doing it in his presence," he said to her just before dozing off. "He's my brother and I love him the same as you."

LITTLE DOV woke at six in the morning; he got up quietly, without waking Esther, covered her with the sheet, and, shoes in hand, tiptoed to the front door to pick up the bottle of milk and bring it to the kitchen. He put the water on to boil for coffee and hunched over the stove, his shoes in one hand, the morning paper in the other, waiting for the kettle to start rumbling. The water was beginning to boil when his brother appeared.

"Sleep well?" Little Dov asked him.

"I took some sleeping pills I found," Dov said. "For a man who rarely sleeps I slept like a log. Only my head is still woozy from the pills."

"That'll pass when you have some coffee," Little Dov said. "Did you see a doctor?"

"What for? Is a doctor gonna slip into my bed at night and play with me, so I'll fall asleep more easily?" He poured himself a cup of coffee and carried it over to the kitchen table. He looked out the window at the red, dusty earth and the bay reflecting the sun; its glare was so bright his eyes began to hurt. "Aren't you late today?" he said. "What about all those stories you hear about fishermen getting up before dawn?"

"I overslept," Little Dov said. "I didn't set the alarm clock so it wouldn't wake you."

"It's not the alarm clock but my jeep that's to blame," Dov said. "I won't let you borrow it again. You need your rest. I know you, sweetie. You don't like to waste the night on sleep."

"I love her," his brother said. "That's why I married her."

"Good," Dov said. "I'll drive you to your boat. Then I'll go to the airport. What time does the first plane land?"

"Seven sharp. But there won't be any tourists on it. They catch later planes. Or they take the bus from Be'er Sheva."

"Doesn't matter," Dov said. "I'll talk to this guy who's supposed to help me."

"Can we leave right now, Dov?"

"Yes. Let me just find my sunglasses."

He got up and went to their room. Israel was still sleeping; he stepped over him, picked up the canvas bag, set it on the table, and began to go through it. Finally, he found a pair of cheap sunglasses and placed them on his forehead. He walked over to the bed and shook Esther gently awake. She opened her eyes and covered herself with the sheet.

"Esther," he said softly, "tell Israel I'll be back around ten. Tell him I've gone to the airport to talk to that guy who's supposed to help us."

"Okay," she whispered. "But why don't you wake him up and tell him yourself?"

He moved his mouth closer to her ear. "I want him to sleep as long as he can. You fall asleep more easily than we do. You have a cleaner conscience."

The two brothers left the house and climbed into the jeep. They drove fast along the empty highway. When they were about to turn left toward the beach, they saw an army truck coming at them from the direction of the airport; Dov braked with his foot, but the jeep didn't slow down; he had to use the hand brake to stop the car.

"What's wrong, Dov?"

"Brakes," Dov said. "I had some problems with them yesterday, soon after Be'er Sheva. I guess there's air in them. The guy who loaned the jeep to me should've warned me."

"Is it something serious?"

"No. I'll drop you off, and then go to the garage. It

should take no more than an hour to fix them."

"If this jeep was yours, there'd be no such surprises," Little Dov said.

"Sure. Any fool can drive his own car."

They were now going along the wet white sand close to the water's edge; the sea was peaceful and still, but so bright Dov's eyes began to hurt again from the glare, and he had to put his sunglasses on. When he felt his brother touch his arm, he turned his head.

"Look," Little Dov said.

Dov stopped the jeep. Two motorboats were moving quickly away from the shore; they watched the two even white stripes of foamy water which the boats left in their wake.

"I'd kill those guys if I knew how," Little Dov said. "And then I'd go to those whores, their mothers, and tell them their sons are dead."

Dov caught him by the shoulders and pulled him close.

"Let them be," he said. "Nothing should happen to them as long as I'm in Eilat. Because if something does, the police will come and get me, not you. Swear that you won't do anything."

His brother didn't answer.

"Swear that you won't do anything," Dov said again. "Or I'll leave this goddamn town today."

"Okay, I swear," Little Dov said, breaking free and getting out of the car. "What do you want me to swear by? By our Pop, that crazy old fool? Or by your wife that you still love even though she's big with another man's bastard?"

Dov regarded him in silence. There was a grimace on his face, and he was breathing hard through his open mouth.

"Don't do anything while I'm here," he said quietly. "And remember that every man's wife can be turned into a whore. Sometimes it doesn't take much urging. She'll do it herself when things between her and her husband really start falling apart."

"I'm sorry, Dov," his brother said. "You should've hit me."

"Come back safely."

He made a U-turn; the wheels got stuck in the sand, so he reversed gears to free them, spraying sand all over Little Dov, who stood rooted with his head bowed, like a child expecting to be hit. Dov saw his brother's blond head in the rearview mirror until he reached the highway. He drove to the airport and left the jeep in the parking lot on the other side of the runway from the barracks. He crossed the runway, feeling sweat gather on his back and soak his shirt through. The man he wanted to see was sitting at a desk, breathing heavily; his face was contorted as if he were dying, even though three electric fans stood in front of him, filling the room with their soft, gentle hum.

"Good day," Dov said. He picked up one of the fans and directed the stream of cool air at his face.

"It's only your second day in Eilat; soon you'll learn that days are never good around here," the man said.

"Do you have the passenger list?" Dov asked.

"The plane will land at ten-twenty. They told me over the phone there should be some passengers on board." Suddenly he jumped up from his chair, jerked the fan out of Dov's hand, and aimed it at his own sweaty face. "I hope they'll like it here. I hope they'll like it here more than I do."

"I'd like to post some notices," Dov said. "You know: jeep and driver for hire, something like that. Maybe it'll catch somebody's eye."

"You believe that?"

"No," Dov said. "But I'd like to do it nonetheless. Two or three notices, if the authorities won't have any objections."

"I'm sure they'll have plenty of objections," the man said. "Lucky for you, no authorities know exactly where this airport is. All the equipment we have is one windsock and one fire extinguisher. Too bad no plane has ever gone up in flames here yet; if one did, things would improve quickly."

"Okay then, I'll be here at ten. Me or my partner."

"Oh, so you have a partner in this wonderful business? Now all you need is a secretary who speaks six languages."

"Just find me some tourists," Dov said. "Somebody must come here for pleasure, for god's sake! You'll get your share. Now I have to go and get my brakes fixed." He turned around.

"Hey, Dov," the man suddenly called out after him.

"Yeah?"

"You can put up all the notices you want, but if anybody from management asks, I'll say I knew nothing, understand?"

"Sure," Dov said. "I understand. You came here from Europe leaving behind a herring stall or some equally important business. And now you blame Moses for not consulting you as to where to go. Thing is he was ashamed to enter any city leading a rabble of men like you. That's why he went out into the desert."

"You're a Sabra, aren't you?" the man asked.

"That's right," Dov said. "A Sabra."

He bought two cans of corned beef in a store opposite the airport barracks and drove off to the garage. The owner of the garage was standing in the shade, drinking a bottle of beer.

"My brakes don't work," Dov told him. "What should I do?"

"Sell that jeep for scrap metal and ride around in a taxi."

"Listen, wise guy, I'm not feeling well. My head hurts

and my eyes are jumping out of their sockets from the glare. So I'll ask you again: what should I do?"

"Write to Elizabeth Taylor," the owner said. "I hear she's endowed a theater in Tel Aviv. Maybe she'll want to help you too. She might even adopt you."

Dov grabbed the bottle the man was holding, tore it out of his grasp and splashed beer in his face; the man jumped back into the shade.

"A little work will do you good and your wife will love you all the more for it," Dov said. "I need that car in two hours. And I want those brakes fixed so good they'll last me until winter."

"I can't use the pit now," the owner of the garage said. "Some men are in it. Go talk to them. They should be finishing soon."

Dov tossed the beer bottle back to him; the man caught it deftly. Dov walked into the garage. When his eyes adapted to the dark, he saw three men and an army GMC truck parked over the pit. The left back wheel was off; one of the men was placing a new bearing in the exposed axle, using a piece of pipe and a wooden hammer.

"Will you be finishing soon?" Dov asked.

The kneeling man turned his face up to him; there were bandages on it, and one of his eyes was swollen. "Yes," he said. "If only this goddamn pit wasn't so shallow! I would have finished long ago if there was a proper car hoist here."

"Is there any other garage in town?" Dov asked.

"No. Be grateful for this dump. At least you can grease the chassis once in a while. My problem is I can't fit my body into a pit this small." There was a proud note in his voice. "I'm too fat and too tall."

"Maybe you're not too tall," Dov said. "Maybe you're a short chap, only your legs are long."

The man looked at him again. "Yeah, maybe you're right," he said. "You're Dov Ben Dov, aren't you?"

Dov opened one of the cans of corned beef and began eating its contents with his knife. "That could be me," he said, pausing between bites. "Though you might have in mind my brother or my eighty-year-old father."

"No, I mean you. I met your brother yesterday evening at the beach."

"It must have been night."

"What does it matter? The important thing is that we met."

"Maybe you interrupted something he was doing?" Dov asked, and the man lifted his hand to his blackened eye. "Something he enjoys doing very much? You don't know my brother. I do. And let me tell you something: his prick is his Achilles heel."

"It's you I wanted to speak to, not your brother."

"What about?"

"I wanted to ask you to tell your brother that hitting people is not nice."

"He knows that," Dov said. He speared another piece of corned beef with his knife and shoved it into his mouth. "I've been telling him that all his life."

"Then you agree, Dov?"

"Agree with what, old bean?"

"That it's not nice to hit people."

"Yes," Dov said. "Absolutely. God, this corned beef tastes awful."

"So you've changed, Dov," the other said. "Even though it's not easy to change when a man's turning forty." He tossed his pipe and mallet to the ground, wiped his hands on a rag, and got to his feet. "Or maybe you haven't? Maybe you say that just because you're on parole and you don't want to get into any trouble?"

"You have a head on your shoulders, so figure it out for yourself. Thinking is difficult at first, but once you get into the habit it can be real fun."

"I guess you haven't changed at all, Dov Ben Dov," the

man said. "That corned beef must be salty, no? You can have some of my beer."

Dov took the offered bottle, raised it to his lips, and took a long swig. "Have you ever met me before?" he asked.

"No, but I know guys who did. In Haifa, Tel Aviv, Jerusalem." He paused. "And even in Akko."

"In Akko?" Dov asked.

"Yes," the other man said. "In Akko."

"Well, well. And what did you think of that jail?"

"I thought it was a very fine jail. Not that I'm in any hurry to get back to it; I didn't find it that special. I came to Eilat straight from there, Dov. I'm not a tourist. If I could choose a different place, I would."

"How long do you have to stay here?"

"Five years. Five long years. Some guys start losing their hair and teeth after two years here, Dov. I'm not a young man anymore. It's hard for me to live under police supervision. We have to live peacefully, whether we like it or not. It's easy to make trouble for guys like you and me. Anybody can do it. Anybody who wants to. Any silly little thing is enough. And then the judge says: The conditional release hasn't worked so it must be revoked. That's what I'm afraid of. Many guys here in Eilat are."

"You need to tell me this?"

"I wish your brother was like you. But he's young and hot-blooded. His young body has quickly adjusted itself to the local conditions. Five years from now he'll still have his own hair and teeth. And he doesn't even have to take any salt pills. Want some more beer, Dov?"

"Yes," Dov said. He reached for the bottle the man held out to him, but instead of taking it, he raised his hand and touched the man's face. "What did you do? Get drunk and start counting stairs with your face?" he asked, and only then took the bottle.

"No," the man said. "Though I wish that were true.

I wish I could say that. I can't. It was your brother; he slugged me a couple of times yesterday. And I couldn't hit him back, just like you couldn't have if somebody had slugged you, right, Dov?" Big and fat, he walked up to Dov, moving with an effort, and stopped half a yard away from him, his hand raised in the air. "Right, Dov?"

"Right," Dov said. "I couldn't have."

"Even if he had called your mother a whore?"

"Yes, even then."

"Even if he had said you're a worthless bum," the man continued, his hand still high in the air, "an officer stripped of his rank and booted out of the army, a man left by his wife, a man whom nobody in the whole country trusts enough to lend one measly pound?"

"Yes," Dov said.

"What if he said your wife had started whoring around and would soon give birth to somebody's bastard? If somebody came up to you and said all those things, would you hit him?"

"No, I wouldn't," Dov said.

"You and I are in the same position," the other said. "You know why I didn't hit your brother last night. But I don't hold a grudge against him. I even want to do something for him."

"Like what?" Dov asked.

"I want to lend him some money."

"He doesn't need it," Dov said. "He has to live on what he makes himself."

"He'll need it to pay his way," the man said. "So he can leave Eilat and go wherever he wants. I'm afraid, Dov. I'm afraid one day he'll provoke me so much that I'll forget myself and hit him. And you know what that would mean for me. Tell him to leave Eilat; tell him I'm ready to help him. He can pay me back when he gets rich. I can wait."

"He won't leave Eilat," Dov said. "And he doesn't need your money."

"I advise him to leave, Dov."

"He doesn't need your advice either. He's got a father and an older brother."

"I want him to leave Eilat," the man said. "I don't like looking at a man who's hit me in the face."

"He's losing his livelihood because of you," Dov said. "You can't expect him to like you."

"Dov, your brother is young and strong. He can fish from a rowboat. I'm twice as old as he is. And I spent five years in a German camp before coming here. I wanted to make some money, enough to survive on without having to look up to people or cater to them. So I did something I shouldn't have. I got caught and landed in jail. Now all I want is to live in peace. It's not my fault I'm not as young as your brother." He paused and then went on. "Tell him to leave Eilat, Dov. For five years men hit me in the face and I had to bear it. I had to look at them day after day. But I won't bear that here in Israel. I don't want to see your brother ever again. Tell him to leave." He turned to the other two men who were standing some distance away and said, "I've finished! I need your help now!"

He and one of the other men tried to lift the wheel and put it back on the axle; their necks and arms turned red from the strain, but their efforts were unsuccessful.

"No way," one of them gasped. "We need two pipes and some bricks."

Dov had been standing motionless; now he tossed away the half-full can of corned beef. The men turned quickly in his direction. They looked at his pale, sweaty face and his joined eyebrows. He walked up to them and pushed them gently away, then dropped to one knee, lifted the wheel and placed it on the axle.

He got to his feet, breathing hard, and wiped his hands on an oily rag. Then he turned to the men; they backed away from him. But he just stood there, catching his breath.

"Forget the bricks and pipes," he said. "The trouble with this pit is that it's much too shallow. Can you move your truck out now so he can bring in my jeep?" He turned to the garage owner, who'd come in, the beer bottle still in his hand. "Get going on my brakes, okay? I'll be back in an hour." He was almost out the door, half a step away from the glare and sunlight, when suddenly he stopped. "My brother was born in this country," he said. "He has a right to live wherever he wants and do whatever he likes." He wiped the sweat off his brow and strode out into the glare and dust.

Israel had almost finished shaving when Esther entered the kitchen. He turned to her.

"I borrowed your mirror," he said. "I took it without asking because I didn't want to wake you up."

She held out two leather wrist straps. "You forgot these," she said.

He took them from her and shoved them into his pocket quickly and savagely.

"I wasn't going to steal them," she said. "I gave them back to you, didn't I?"

"Where did you find them?"

"On the table."

"They're not mine," he said. "They're Dov's." He took them out of his pocket and looked at them for a moment; then he put them back.

"Did Dov tell you where he was going?"

"He said he'd be back around ten," Esther said. "He said something about going to the airport. They left together. Dov and Dov." She touched Israel's shoulder, and he spun around; half of his face was still covered with soap. "What do you think? Will he help us?"

"With what?"

"Will he do something about those men?"

"Esther," Israel said, "Dov isn't twenty anymore. He's tired."

"Well, I'm twenty," Esther said. "I have the right to expect something more from life. I spent two years in the army, then I married my Dov." She fell silent and stood there, leaning against the window ledge. He could see a drop of sweat at the base of her short, straight nose. "I only see him at night," she said. "He's always worked like a horse, but then those men came here and nobody wants to help him."

"Dov is tired," Israel said. "He didn't have an easy life. And now he can't take any risks."

They heard heavy footsteps in the hall and turned around; Dov's father stood in the doorway.

"Yes," the old man said. "He won't take any risks. He burned everything behind him and came here like a worthless bum to eat his brother's bread. He's not too old for that, and he knew he was not risking anything by coming here; he knew his brother loved him and would share his last piece of bread with him."

"And what do you think he should do about those men?" Israel asked.

"What's done, or should be done, with thieves," the old man said. "No matter what people think."

"I hate violence," Israel said. "I came here so that I'd never have to look at it again."

"I see," the old man said. "You came here so you'd never again have to look upon violence. Beautifully said, Israel." He took a step toward him. "Do you think the men who came here before you had this country handed to them on a plate?" he asked. "No, Israel. Nobody gave it to them. To take it, they had to resort to violence, and the best of them died doing it, as usually happens. How can you, a Jew, speak to me of violence?"

"You're an old and religious man," Israel said. "It wouldn't be proper for me to argue with you."

"You wouldn't know how to," the old man said. He stepped up to Israel and took him by the arm. Israel shivered. Although it was almost a hundred and forty degrees, the old man's hand was cool and dry.

"Look at him, Esther," the old man said. "He's unique. He should like violence. All weak men do."

"Do you want some tea, Pop?" Esther asked.

"No," the old man said. "I want you to look at him. Look at him, Esther." He watched her in silence, his lined face twitching slightly; he continued to hold Israel's arm in his bony hand. "I asked you to look at him, Esther," he said again.

She turned her head and regarded Israel. Her expression didn't change; her gaze was intent, but indifferent.

"Would you want him for your husband, Esther?"

"I already have a husband, Pop," Esther said quietly. "That's the only answer I can give you."

"Would you like to have him in your bed, Esther?" the old man asked. "Look at his arms, Esther. I bet I'm stronger than he is." The cool hand tightened its grip on Israel's arm. "Would you go to bed with him, Esther, if you didn't have a husband and could do whatever you liked?"

Once again she fixed her eyes on Israel, and they studied each other. She gazed at his tired, alert, and handsome face; he stared at her thick hair and strong, brown neck.

"No," she said.

The old man released Israel's arm and patted Esther's cheek. "You're a good child, Esther," he said. "I'm sorry it is one of my sons that will ruin your life."

"Does a man have to believe in violence and beat up people to deserve respect?" Israel asked.

"No," the old man said. "He doesn't. He can die like all good Jews did." He turned around and began to walk away. When he reached the doorway, he stopped and faced them again; and again they saw his wrinkled face and his madman's eyes. "Why don't you have a child, Esther?" he asked suddenly.

"We've been married only three months, Pop," Esther said, not looking at either of them. "We thought we would wait awhile—"

"I can't wait," the old man said impatiently. "I'm eighty years old, Esther. At this age every day is a gift from God. I want to see my grandsons before I die. My older son won't have any children, so it is my younger son's duty to give me that joy. I'll ask you again a month from now,

Esther. Remember, I love you like my own daughter."

"Yes, Pop," she said. She stepped up to him. "Pop, I want to ask you something."

"Yes, Esther?"

"What will happen to Dina, Dov's wife?"

"Nothing, Esther," the old man said. "Nothing happens to women throughout their lives. They come into this world and they die unchanged."

"But what do you think should happen to her, Pop?"

"I don't know, Esther. You heard what my son said. He came to me and said his wife was going to give birth to a bastard." He paused. "When I was a kid, my father bought a German shepherd bitch. But he didn't keep a close watch on her and one day she was covered by a mongrel. When she whelped, we went to the river and drowned the pups. And the next day my father took the bitch and his gun and went to the woods. He never told me what he did with her. What d'you think?"

"Your father was a wise man, Pop," Esther said. "That's what I think."

"So do I," Dov's father said and went out into the hall. They listened to the heavy tread of his receding footsteps, and then they heard his quiet, monotonous voice; he had begun to pray.

"You don't have an easy life with him here," Israel said. He was still looking at Esther, at her strong neck and thick eyebrows, which came together above her nose, just like Dov's.

"You won't either," she said.

"Dov was right," Israel said softly. "He's cruel like a child. Like every old person, like my mother."

"Where's your mother now?"

"I don't know," he said. "I just know where I buried her."

They heard through the window the roar of the jeep's engine and the squeal of brakes; a moment later Dov marched into the kitchen. He took off his shirt and threw it on the floor.

"Go to the airport, Israel," he said. "I had the brakes fixed; they should work fine now. The plane's landing in a few minutes."

"I wish you'd go the first time," Israel said.

"Yeah, I know," Dov said. "But I want you to go. Maybe you'll turn my luck."

"Listen, Dov—"

Dov reached into his pocket for the car keys and tossed them to him. "The plane's coming."

"Dov," Israel said, "I think they're right, all those people who feel we shouldn't stick together. Your father is right, your brother is right, and so was the fat guy who lent you his jeep. I don't believe I can turn your luck." He went up to Dov, who had lowered himself into a chair, and looked at his heavy brown shoulders, glistening with sweat. "I'll go back to Tel Aviv, Dov. I'll find myself a job there."

"You won't find one," Dov said. "You couldn't find one before."

"Nobody will ever like me as long as I tag along with you," Israel said. "You know that. They all think I'm a burden to you. The worst thing is, I've begun to think so myself. Maybe I was afraid to admit it until now." When Dov remained silent, he said, "Yes, I was afraid to admit it. I was too weak even to admit that."

"The plane's landing any minute now," Dov said. "Get moving, Israel. Nobody's going to pay us for sitting on our butts."

Israel stepped to the door. He stopped and once again looked at Dov, who was sitting motionless, breathing hard, his arms lowered, a grimace on his face.

"Remember what I told you," Israel said.

"What was that?"

"I don't believe I can ever turn your luck, and nobody's

going to like me as long as I tag along with you."

"It's too hot for me to rack my brain over people's likes and dislikes," Dov said. "Find me a simpler problem."

"Israel is right," Esther said.

They both turned to her.

"Anybody ask your opinion, Esther?" Dov said.

"No," she said. "You're just like your brother. Neither of you has ever asked for my opinion. You love only each other. Dov loves Dov, Dov admires Dov, and Dov listens only to what Dov says. You need women only between ten in the evening and six in the morning, and only for one reason: so you'll fall asleep more easily and dream of each other. But I shouldn't be telling you all that. I should be listening to what you're saying so that I can repeat it all later to my Dov and finally hold his attention."

She walked past Israel. As he moved out of her way, he felt the heat from her body. She left the kitchen, softly closing the door.

"See?" Israel said.

"She shouldn't have opened her trap," Dov said. "I'm surprised my brother never taught her better. Look, the problem is not you; the problem is me and my unwillingness to get involved in their squabble with those fishermen. I won't get involved. They can talk themselves blue in the face; it won't help." He gave Israel his sunglasses. "Forget the whole thing."

"They won't."

"Now go to the airport and try to pick up a tourist," Dov said. "If you see a Jew in a suit with a camera in his hand, walk up to him and be ready to bargain about the price, because he'll never pay as much as you ask. Since you'll probably be talking in English, at some point just say to him, Man, I need the gelt. He should understand; if he does, take him where he wants to go. If he looks like a religious man, charge him double."

"Will you remember what I said?"

"No, I've already forgotten. It's a hundred and forty degrees outdoors and probably more inside. People who live here have to take salt pills because if they don't, their bones snap like twigs. If we stay here two years longer, we'll lose all our teeth and hair. We'll never look like those actors who play sons of the desert and heroes of the tropics. I'm sorry, Israel. I'm locked up in my body as if it were a cage nobody's going to open until my death. That's all I can think about. Or maybe I can't. Maybe it just seems to me that I'm thinking. There'll be no rain here until the end of October."

"Yes," Israel said. "Or even until the end of November."

He stood for a moment in the doorway staring at Dov who continued to sit inert, his eyes closed, breathing hard. Sitting like that in the glare coming through the window, naked to the waist, he looked like a blind man. The shirt he had thrown down on the floor was still there, though he had moved it with his foot; a wet mark on the tiles showed where it had first landed. Dov's heavy body didn't budge when Israel finally left, slamming the door.

NEARING THE AIRPORT, HE COULD SEE THE DAKOTA coming over the mountain range; he waited in the jeep by the airport gate on which somebody had placed a broken sign with the crookedly lettered message NO TRESPASSING; he watched the plane describe an arc over the bay, where the flat roofs of Aqaba glimmered faintly in the white sun; then the plane landed heavily, raising clouds of reddish dust. He watched the passengers descend and begin walking toward the gate, grimacing and narrowing their eyes against the sun: two young men carrying scuba gear, and an old woman accompanied by an old man, probably her husband, whom she clutched by the arm, yelling something into his ear. Then one more woman left the plane and stopped helplessly on the runway, dazed by the glare and the heat; a moment later the stewardess swung the door shut.

The old woman and her husband approached Israel.

"Will you take us to a hotel?"

"That's why I'm here," he said. "To take people where they want to go. Have you got a room reservation? If not, I can take you to the Eilat Hotel."

The old woman glanced at her husband, tall and thin and ramrod straight; the earpiece of a hearing aid was stuck in his ear, while the microphone dangled from his hand; he was playing with it as if it were the pendant on the waist chain of an old-fashioned watch.

"I didn't say I wanted to squander my money," she said. "They told me at the tourist office how much that hotel costs. We can stay at a cheaper one. We want to wash after the trip and then go see the sights. We're leaving on the afternoon plane."

"Okay," Israel said.

56

"How much do you charge?"

"It depends on how long you want the jeep for."

"For three hours," she said. "We'd like to see King Solomon's mines and whatever else of interest there is here."

"What about a drive around the desert?"

"No," she said. "We saw it from the plane. You don't expect anyone to pay for looking at sand, do you?"

"Then it'll be twenty pounds," Israel said.

"That's too much."

"Give him the money," the old man wheezed.

Israel watched the woman as she raised her hand to her husband's ear and pulled his earpiece out.

"He was never any good at doing business," she said. "His brothers cheated him all his life, and now he's come here to squander away all I managed to save."

"I can't hear anything," the old man screeched. He groped for his earpiece, but the woman pushed his hand away.

"Twenty pounds," Israel said.

"That's robbery," she said. "They told me at the tourist office that it costs twenty pounds to rent a jeep for the whole day; we want it for only three hours!"

"This is the only plane," Israel said. "And none of the locals want to go sightseeing. Most of them would pay through the nose just to leave Eilat."

"I want to see King Solomon's mines," the old man screeched again. "Give him the twenty pounds."

"No," the woman said. She stuck the earpiece back in her husband's ear and leaned against the jeep's hood, intending to go on haggling about the price. Suddenly she jumped away, her face twisted with shock and pain.

"It's a hundred and forty degrees now," Israel said. "Didn't they tell you that at the tourist office?"

"I'll take the jeep," a woman behind him suddenly said. He didn't see her; he only heard her voice reaching him through walls of heat, and he thought with reluctance that he would have to turn around and face her.

"Twenty pounds," he said, without turning around.

"I know," she said. "I heard you say it three times. The first two times I didn't say anything, but now I'm joining in. Like at an auction."

"What auction?" the old man screeched.

Israel turned around. The woman was standing a few steps away, smoking a cigarette.

"Oh, it's you," he said. "I saw you leave the plane. You want me to take you to a hotel?"

She walked over and he helped her get into the jeep.

"I heard one could rent a room privately," she said. "That there are people here who take in lodgers. Would you know of anyone?"

"I can find out," he said. "Then what?"

"I'd like to see all there's to be seen in Eilat," she said. "That's why I came here. But I don't have much time."

"How long do you plan to stay?"

"Three days," she said. "Then I have to go back." She looked at the old couple walking slowly in the sun. "Can we give them a lift? That woman looks as if she's going to drop any moment."

"My mother died in this country," he said, throwing the car into gear. "It says on her tombstone: Here lies Sarah, Mordechai's daughter, a God-fearing old woman who has gone the way of all flesh." He turned to the woman. "It would be best for this old hag if she also died. Right here, in this country, which she probably detests. There'd be less sorrow in the world then."

"And what about me?" she asked.

"Well, what about you?"

"I'm over thirty," she said. "Can I live a few more years?"

"I don't know," he said. "It depends on you."

"Well, can you find out?"

"Sure," he said. "I'll tell you before you leave."

"You have three days to gather the information," she said. "And now stop the jeep. I want you to give this old couple a lift. I'll pay you for it."

He accelerated and drove past the old couple, covering them with sand. He continued to step on the gas until the arrow of the speedometer moved lazily from forty to fifty, and then he braked hard and jumped out of the jeep. They were midway between the airport and the main highway and nobody could see them. He circled the hood and stopped by the woman's side.

"Listen," he said, "I won't give that old hag a lift. Not even for forty pounds. That's why I asked her for twenty pounds; I didn't want her to ride in this jeep. Anybody else I would have charged ten. And that's how much I'll charge you for three hours."

"What have you got against her? She hasn't done you any harm."

"She reminds me of someone I want to forget," he said.

"You should stop having affairs with girls well past their menopause. You'll save yourself lots of trouble."

"She reminds me of my mother."

"I'm sorry," she said and held out her hand, but he ignored it. He stood still and the red dust settled slowly over his sweaty face. After a while he took a moist cigarette out of his shirt pocket and lit it.

"Can we drive on?" he asked.

"Yes," she said. "First we'll find that room for me, okay?"

"Sure," he said. "Everything is fine now." He got back behind the wheel and started off. In the rear-view mirror he could see the old couple shuffling slowly along in the direction of the highway; he knew that she also was watching them in the mirror. But he didn't stop; he drove on quickly, raising clouds of red dust that soon obscured the old couple, outlandish and out of place in their black clothes, so much in discord with the mountains, the white sun, and the tranquil bay. He reached the main highway and turned right toward the town. He spat out the cigarette butt and looked at his passenger. For a moment he gazed in silence at her slim, weary face.

"I, too, will die here," he said finally, lighting a new cigarette. "No doubt about it. It's much too hot here for someone born in Europe. Just imagine, it'll be like this, with no rain, for the next five months—" He glanced at her again. "I'll stop by the place where I'm staying and ask about a room for you. They might know of something."

"Okay," she said. "It doesn't have to be anything special. Just a clean room for three days."

He stopped the jeep in front of Little Dov's house and walked inside. Esther was asleep; Dov was sitting by the window reading a newspaper.

"Hey, Dov," Israel whispered. "Come out to the kitchen."

Dov left the room, closing the door behind him.

"There's this woman who's looking for a place to stay," Israel said. "Can you help? I've just picked her up at the airport. Maybe you know of someone who'd want to rent a room for three days?"

"We can try the neighbors," Dov said. "If she doesn't expect us to pay her rent, that is. I hope you've made it clear that you won't be driving her around Eilat just for the fun of it."

"I told her it'd be my pleasure to take her wherever she wants to go as long as she pays for it," Israel said.

They crossed the yard and knocked on the door of a house that looked exactly the same as Little Dov's. A fat woman opened the door.

"Do you want to rent a room?" Dov asked. "There's a woman, a tourist, who's looking for a room for three days."

"Three days? Is it worth it?" the fat woman asked.

"I don't know," Israel said. "Say yes or no."

"My, my, aren't we impatient? Is she alone?"

"Yes."

"How much does she want to pay?"

"Ten pounds a day," Israel said. "That's the going rate for rooms around here."

"She'll bring in men," the fat woman said grudgingly.

"You haven't even seen her, so how can you know?" Dov said. "And even if she does, what do you care? The important thing is she won't bring in women. At least men don't get pregnant. Well?"

"Okay, but she has to pay me in advance," the fat woman said.

"I think she'll agree to that," Israel said. "I'll go and ask her. And if she wants to see the room, I'll bring her over."

"One moment," the fat woman said, looking at them as if she suddenly woke up from a dream. "Who are you, the two of you?"

"I'm Dov Ben Dov," Dov said. "And this is my friend Israel. Satisfied?"

"You're Dov Ben Dov?" she asked. "I already know two men by that name."

"I'm the third one," Dov said. "The worst one. The one you heard all the stories about. We'll be back in a minute."

They went to the jeep.

"This is my friend, Dov Ben Dov," Israel said. "He helped me find you a room."

"Ben Dov," the woman said. "In Hebrew this means the son of—I've forgotten. God, I knew that word, but now it's slipped my mind."

"Bear, son of Bear," Dov said. "A very nice name, considering that no one has ever seen a bear in this country."

"Yes," she said, holding out her hand. "And my name is Ursula. People address each other by their first names here, no?"

"It's more convenient that way," Dov said. "I know a guy who's named Moses Treppengelander. And another one who's named Samuel Paradiserweg. Who'd want to say all that?"

"You were born here," she said, fixing her eyes on him.

"Yes, in Haifa," he said. "How did you know I was born in Israel?"

"I just knew it," she said, staring at his heavy shoulders. "And you do look like a bear."

He took a step in her direction. His face remained expressionless, only the spot where his eyebrows joined seemed to thicken suddenly.

"Has anybody ever told you what you look like? What kind of woman?" he asked. Then he turned and walked away.

"It's best to leave him alone," Israel said. "He can be very unpleasant."

"Did I offend him in some way?" she asked.

"No," Israel said. "Nobody needs to offend him. That's the trouble. It's enough that he imagines the whole world is trying to offend him. There are people like that, you know." He took her suitcase from the back seat. "Let's go and see that room. It'll cost you half of what a hotel room would."

She didn't move. She was still watching the door behind which Dov had disappeared.

"That man has insulted me," she said quietly. "Even though I did him no wrong. I've barely been in this town fifteen minutes."

"One often pays for the wrongs done by others," Israel said. "Every Jew ought to know that. Hasn't your mother ever told you that?"

"I'm sorry, but I'm not Jewish," she said. "My husband was a Jew. That's why I came here, to see the things he told me so much about. I didn't come here to be insulted."

"Dov won't change," Israel said. "I can apologize for him if you want me to."

"My husband told me that when you welcome somebody in Hebrew, you say, Blessed be the one who cometh hither. Doesn't anybody say these words anymore?"

"Of course they do," Israel said. "Plenty of people say them. And feel that way about strangers. Actually, I don't know anybody who doesn't. And of all the people I know, Dov is usually the one most likely to."

He moved off, carrying her suitcase; after a moment, Ursula got out of the jeep and followed. They crossed the yard and approached the fat woman's house; the fat woman herself was still standing in the doorway.

"Let's see that room," Israel said. He walked in, shouldering her aside.

The room she showed them was bright and clean.

"You won't find a room like this for fifteen pounds anywhere else," she said. "I'm renting it only because my husband—"

"For fifteen pounds we don't want it," Israel said. "You settled for ten."

"Ten? I think you have trouble understanding Hebrew. How long have you been in this country?"

"You said ten," Israel said.

"There must be some mistake. Ask your friend. If Dov Ben Dov says I settled for ten, I'll agree. My loss. I don't need to make a profit. Others die of hunger, so I can suffer a loss. It won't kill me. But ask Dov Ben Dov. I want to hear it from his mouth."

"Dov has said too many things for which he later had to appear in court," Israel said. "It's best to leave him alone."

"You want to ruin me!"

"No, I don't," Israel said, picking up the suitcase he had already placed on the bed. "We'll find a different room."

"Did I say no?" the fat woman asked. "Did I say you can't have it? Let it be my loss." She turned to Ursula who was still standing in the door. "What is it, dear? You look depressed."

"No," Ursula said, "I'm just tired. And hot."

"I'll make you some coffee, dear," the fat woman said. "Coffee is what keeps one alive here."

"Right," Israel said. "Then it's settled. Wash up and have some coffee. I'll go home and drink something too. When you're ready, just honk the horn. I'll leave the keys in the jeep."

Back home, he took a bottle of beer out of the refrigerator in the kitchen and walked into the room. His hands trembled with anger as he poured the beer into a glass.

"You have some strange ideas about making money, Dov," he said. "Most people are really odd; they don't like being insulted."

"Did he say something rude to her?" Esther asked; she was still rosy from sleep, like a child.

"Not at all," Israel said. "He only implied she looked like a whore. Apart from that, he was really charming. If she spoke Hebrew better, she'd have told him he was very sweet. The reason she didn't is that her Hebrew isn't too good."

"Dov was right," Esther said.

Israel turned to her. "Why was he right?" he asked. "Who gave him the right to insult somebody he's never met before?"

"I saw the way she was looking at him," Esther said.

"And how was that, if you don't mind telling me?" Israel asked.

"As if there was something about him she didn't like," Esther said.

"Like what?"

"His clothes," Esther said.

"Don't try to defend me, Esther," Dov said. "The best lawyers in this country tried, but in the end they always lost the case."

"You don't need anybody to defend you," Esther said. "And nobody could do it."

"Then what do I need, Esther?" Dov asked.

"You need somebody who'd love you," Esther said. "Though I doubt anyone would know how."

"This is the second time today you're meddling in my affairs," Dov said. "I haven't asked for your opinion."

"That woman hasn't asked for yours either," Esther said. "She was just sitting in the jeep and looking at you. And I happened to be standing by the window and saw it all."

"Esther," Dov said, "I have enough troubles as it is. Don't add to them. Stand by the window, stand on your head, stand where you like, but leave me alone."

"Look, it wasn't me that was looking at you." She regarded him for a moment in a stony, unfriendly fashion. "And it wasn't me that didn't like your clothes," she added, storming out of the kitchen.

"There's one thing she forgot to say," Israel said.

"What is that?"

"That she could have moved away from the window. Or turned around and looked at something else. At this picture of your brother in uniform, for instance." He stepped up to the wall and pointed at a picture of Little Dov that hung there in a coral frame. It had been taken when Little Dov was serving his time in the army; he was dressed in a paratrooper's uniform. "She could have looked at this picture. But she didn't."

"Are you implying something, Israel?" Dov asked. "Don't forget she's my brother's wife."

Israel turned to Dov and looked at him in silence. He smiled, but his eyes remained hard.

"I hope she is not forgetting that," he said after a pause.

He pointed again at the picture. "It must be a recent one. Esther and Dov met in the army, didn't they?"

"Listen, Israel," Dov said. "Esther was born in this country like me and my brother. She has learned to speak her mind. Nobody should hold that against her."

"I understand," Israel said. "What you're saying is that you who were born here are different from the rest of us. Different meaning better." He heard the blare of the jeep's horn and placed the glass of beer he was holding on the kitchen table. "I have to go," he said. "I'll drive her around Eilat and then come back. And I'll apologize to her for you."

"Don't," Dov said. "I didn't mean to insult her. I have no idea how it happened."

"I will," Israel said. "You know why? Because I'm afraid that you may suddenly decide to apologize to her in person. And that would be the worst thing that could happen, Dov. Because the worst thing is not that you offend people or get into fights; it's that later you want to apologize to them. That's when the real trouble starts. And that's what I'm afraid of."

They heard the jeep's horn again and Israel walked out. Dov got up, went to the window, and looked at Israel and Ursula. Then he turned around and looked at his brother's picture and saw that it was somewhat askew. Israel must have shifted it a little, because the wall was slightly paler along one side of the frame. He stared for a moment at the picture, at his brother's eyes, which watched him mirthlessly, at his blond hair sticking out from under the paratrooper's cap, then he stepped up to the wall and moved the frame into place.

URSULA WAS ALREADY SITTING IN THE JEEP. SHE HAD put on a pair of somewhat dirty blue jeans. Israel smiled at her, then looked down at his own pants; they were exactly the same shade of blue and just as dirty.

"Where shall we go first?"

"I have no idea," she said. "What's worth seeing around here? You must know."

"Well, there's my friend Dov," Israel said. "But you already saw him. We could drive to the beach and rent a boat with a glass bottom through which you can watch fish and other stuff."

"And what else?"

"The problem is, I don't know," he said. "I don't know Eilat. It's only my second day here. And I already hate the place."

"You're a strange guide," she said. "I won't be in the least surprised if you tell me next that you don't have a driver's license and this jeep doesn't belong to you."

"Of course it doesn't belong to me," he said. "I don't think I'll ever be rich enough to drive a car of my own. But that doesn't mean we can't go sightseeing. I'm just as curious as you are about this goddamn town."

"Okay, let's go to the beach," she said, "and check out those boats with the glass bottoms. As long as I'm here I'd like to see something of Eilat. Though I must have begun touring the country from the wrong end."

"You've never been to Israel before?"

"No," she said. "I know only what my husband told me. Though he had never been here himself."

"He's dead now?"

"He died two years ago," she said.

Israel stopped the jeep and turned his face to her.

Sweat was running down his brow and getting into his eyes; he wiped it off with his hand, but that didn't seem to help much.

"Listen," he said, "you don't have to pay me. Why don't you see this town on your own? Half an hour would be enough. You really don't have to pay me that ten pounds." He paused. "I wouldn't want you to think that someone was trying to swindle you. Here, in this country your husband told you so much about. It's a country like any other. And the people here are no different from other people." When she didn't say anything, he asked, "You're German, aren't you?"

"Yes," she said. "You guessed by my accent?"

"I don't know," he said. "I can always tell Germans. I think I would be able to recognize them in the dark and even if they didn't say a word."

"Do you mind that I'm a German?"

"No," he said. "Germans never got in the way of Jews. It was always the other way around. Didn't your husband tell you that?"

"I want to see this country," she said stubbornly. "I want to see everything my husband told me about. That's why I came here."

"Okay," Israel said. He started the jeep and they drove toward the bay. "I don't know Eilat, so maybe you can show it to me. I guess you could call me a *cicerone à rebours*. But I never expected anybody would want to pay me for something like this."

"Well, I do," she said. "You can like Germans or not, but Germans always pay."

"There are many people in Israel who have refused all war reparations," he said. "Nobody in the world knows how much exactly he should get for his mother's murder. Or for the loss of an eye. Or for spending five years in a concentration camp. Maybe that's why those people don't want to accept money that's rightfully theirs. Or maybe they think the rates will go up with time and they're afraid of accepting too little."

She turned to him.

"I can't say anything about that," she said. "I came here to see the country my husband told me so much about." She looked ahead at the red, dusty road; a layer of dust had already settled on her slim, weary face. "My husband, whom I loved very dearly," she added.

"I'm sorry," Israel said. "I shouldn't have said what I did. After all, my mother died here, in a free country. And I'm free too."

Suddenly he braked hard; she had to brace herself against the windshield with her hand. The jeep stopped.

"What's wrong?" she asked.

He didn't answer; he was watching a plane coming in for a landing from over the bay, its undercarriage half out.

"What a fool," he said loudly.

"Who?"

"That goddamn pilot," he said. "Letting out the undercarriage in the middle of a turn! That's the quickest way to plummet to the ground. Where the hell did he train to be a pilot, in a coal mine? Only a dead drunk miner could have issued him a pilot's license. I haven't seen anything so stupid as long as I live."

"Do you like planes?" she asked.

He didn't answer; he hadn't heard her question. He was still watching the plane. She looked at his hands and saw they were executing strange movements, as if they held something that was invisible but gave resistance, that had to do with the control of a machine's motion; then the plane touched down heavily on the runway, and Israel's hands came to rest on the jeep's steering wheel.

"Were you a pilot?" she asked.

"No," he said. "And I never will be."

He started the car again. They were driving now along

the bay, tranquil and luminous; she turned her gaze toward the sea and the white houses of Aqaba on the other side of the border.

"What's over there?" she asked, pointing.

"I don't know," he said. "It looks like an oil-processing plant or something of the sort."

"You don't like this country, do you?" she asked.

"I dislike Eilat. I never said I disliked Israel. Actually, I've never given that question any serious thought."

"Why did you come here?"

"Because I thought I should," he said. "And it turned out to be an illusion. People should never do things they don't want to do. But there are always others who can make them do something against their will and even talk them into believing it's what they want most themselves."

Israel stopped the jeep. "Here we are," he said. "See that boat out in the bay? That's the one I told you about. They should be back in a few minutes."

"Look!" she said. "There's that old couple you wouldn't give a ride to."

He turned and saw the two people in black garb shuffling slowly along the beach. The woman was still clutching her husband's arm; from time to time she would yell something to him, bringing her mouth to his ear.

"They look as if they're in the wrong movie," Ursula said. "It happens. You are somewhere, maybe doing your shopping, and suddenly you see someone who looks totally out of place. Just as if the projectionist got his rolls of film mixed up."

"Don't worry about them," Israel said. "I'm sure they don't feel the way you do. They are certain their presence is what was lacking here and only now is everything finally in perfect order."

As the old couple strolled by, Israel saw that their eyes were red and glazed from the sun; the old man was walking with his mouth wide open like someone who's breathing his last and will drop dead the next instant.

"That bitch made him come here," Israel said. "She convinced him he should see this country before he died, and then dragged him here all the way from New York or California. Now he can go back and die."

"You don't like old people, do you?"

"No," he said. "How can anybody like them? They know too much and have too little dignity. That old bitch thinks the world couldn't go on without her. That's why she browbeats her travel agent and flies here halfway across the world, spending money that'd be enough to feed five hungry men."

"That woman could be your mother," Ursula said.

"I'd say the same thing about my mother," he said. "Fortunately, my mother is no longer here." For a few moments he watched the old couple trudging slowly and doggedly along, even though each step they took must have required an effort. "Americans never say somebody's dead; they say he's gone or departed. But I prefer to think that old people really die and I'll never see them again. All those old mothers who ruined their children's lives. They won't come back."

"I don't understand that," she said. "My mother died when I was nine. I often wish I could talk to her. Maybe things would have been different if she had lived."

"Oh, definitely," he said. "She would have taken care of that. She would have done everything to ruin your life. But, believe me, none of them ever come back. They don't return, they disappear, together with their despicable bodies, their wisdom, and bad breath. Have you ever thought of how an old woman really smells? Nobody wants to think about it. No animal smells as bad as an old woman."

"Did your mother harm you in some way?"

"The worst thing is she always did everything with my happiness in mind," he said. "She wanted me to come here and live like a free man. I had begun to study aircraft construction and was already in my third year when she came to me and said, Israel, they are letting Jews leave. So what? I asked. Things may change, she said. They may stop doing that. Israel, do something for your mother. Let me die in a free country. She was already ill and knew she'd die soon, but she was determined to die in Israel. So we came here, and my mother died. But I couldn't go on studying aircraft construction. They don't teach it here. And that's the end of my story."

"Can't you leave this country?"

"Where would I go?" he said. "My place is here. I'm a Jew."

"Everybody can live wherever he wants," she said. "You're wrong thinking the way you do. If everyone thought that way, there'd be no American nation. There'd only be Jews, Germans, Portuguese, and God knows who else living in America."

"You've put it all very nicely," he said, "but one needs money to go away and study. Hasn't your husband ever told you about money? It's the only bad thing Jews didn't invent."

"You should leave Israel and continue your studies elsewhere," she said. "You can always come back here later and work in your profession." She paused. "Maybe I could help. My husband had many friends; I could talk to them. Some of them are rich and maybe they'd be willing to do something for you."

"Where are they?"

"In Germany."

He smiled. "That means I'd have to study in Germany, wouldn't I? Germany, of all places! I never thought life could be so amusing. But thanks, anyway."

"Do you hate Germans?"

"No," he said. "I pity them. But pity is worse than hate. What does one feel for people who murdered children? Hate? I believe God has turned His back on Germans once and for all. And that He'll never show His face to them again and will never punish them, even if they commit a thousand new crimes in the future. That's not hate." He looked at his watch. "Where's that goddamn boat? It should have come back long ago."

Someone touched his arm and he turned his head. Two men were standing by the jeep; he and Ursula hadn't noticed their approach.

"You're Ben Dov's friend?" one of the men asked.

"Yes," Israel said.

The man reached into his pocket, took out a wad of bills and held it out to Israel. "Give this money to the younger Ben Dov," he said. "Give it to him and tell him to leave Eilat."

"Did he ask you for it?" Israel asked.

"That's not important," the man said. He removed his sunglasses and gingerly touched the Band-Aid under his eye. "The important thing is that you give him the money and that he goes away."

"Settle it with him yourself," Israel said. "I know nothing about this and I have no intention of getting involved."

"And you know nothing about him slugging me last night?"

"No," Israel said.

"Well, now you do," the second man said. "Take the money Yehuda is offering and give it to young Dov."

"Give it to him yourself," Israel said.

"I don't want to see that bastard again," Yehuda said. "I want him to disappear. If he doesn't, I'll go to the police." He caught Israel's wrist and tried to stick the money in his palm, but Israel pulled his hand away.

"No, I won't take it," he said.

"I'm asking you one last time: take this money and give it to the younger Dov," Yehuda said. "Look, I have nothing against you personally; I prefer to make friends than enemies."

Israel jumped out of the jeep and turned to the two men.

"I know what you want," he said. "But you're not as clever as you think. You could give him the money yourself, but you prefer to pretend you want me to act as the go-between. Because you know I won't take your money. You just want to provoke me into a fight. Because you think that Dov Ben Dov will then come after you, and the police will arrest him and send him away, and then you'll be able to handle his brother without too much trouble. That's your plan, isn't it? But nothing doing. I intend to climb back into my jeep and drive off quietly, and nothing's going to happen."

The second man suddenly slugged him in the jaw; Israel staggered and fell. He got up shakily and leaned against the jeep's hood.

"Nothing doing," he said. "Dov won't go after you. You can hit me again."

The man did; then Yehuda began striking Israel with the fist in which he still clutched the money; Israel again fell to the ground.

"Defend yourself," Ursula screamed at him. She jumped out of the jeep, ran to him, and helped him get up. "Why aren't you defending yourself?"

He pushed her gently aside and wiped his mouth. "Dov won't get involved," he said to the men. "Well, go on. What are you waiting for?"

The second man again slammed him in the mouth, but this time Israel didn't fall. He held onto the steel grid of the jeep's radiator and stood there, a smile on his face. The second man hit him once more.

"Hit him back!" Ursula yelled. "Come on!"

"It won't do you any good," Israel said to the men. "I'll simply forget this ever happened. That's all."

"Remember, we'll meet again," Yehuda said. Then he and the other man walked away.

Ursula watched Israel in silence as he wiped his bloodied lip with the back of his hand, and then suddenly she slapped him in the face as hard as she could. She looked at him in terror like someone suddenly wakened from sleep.

"You don't have to say anything," Israel said.

He got into the jeep with difficulty and rested his head on the steering wheel. Then he took Ursula's bag from the seat and handed it to her. She stood without moving and watched him drive off in a cloud of red dust. He reached the highway and turned right; soon the jeep disappeared from view.

LITTLE DOV WAS WALKING ALONG THE BEACH, HIS RIGHT arm around Esther. In his left hand he was carrying his shirt and shoes; it was so dark he could barely see the waves lapping at his feet. The sky over the bay was invisible and a distant hum was coming from the water.

"Hey," Esther suddenly said, "isn't that your brother's jeep?"

"That's impossible." Little Dov said. "Dov's been looking for Israel all over town. He visited all the bars, asking if anybody's seen him, and now he's ringing up all the hotels. Why should Israel be sitting here on the beach when Dov is going out of his mind with worry?"

They walked up to the jeep; it stood with its lights off at the end of the beach, almost at the Jordanian border. Israel was dozing in the driver's seat, slumped over the steering wheel.

"Hey, wake up," Little Dov said. He had to shake Israel's arm several times before the sleeping man raised his head. "My brother is going out of his mind with worry. He was sure something had happened to you. Go sleep at home."

"Give me a cigarette," Israel said. "I think I've smoked all the ones I had."

Little Dov gave him a cigarette and his lighter. When Israel lit it, they saw in its light that his face was swollen and bruised.

"What happened to your face, Israel?" Little Dov asked. "Did you have an accident?"

"Yes," he said.

"Did you damage the jeep?" Esther asked. When he didn't answer, she walked around the jeep, inspecting it carefully. "Everything looks fine," she said.

"I was driving too fast when I suddenly saw this child," Israel said. "I braked hard and hit my head against the—the—" He fell silent.

"Against what?" Esther asked. She took her husband's lighter and flicked it on Israel's face. He lifted his hand against the light. "What did you hit it against?"

"I hit it, Esther, that's all," he said softly. "Take that goddamn light away. My head hurts."

Little Dov took the lighter from her hand.

"I'm thirsty," Israel said.

"Buy yourself something to drink," Little Dov said. "There's a stand by the hotel where they sell cold beer."

"I haven't got any money," Israel said.

"You spent the whole day driving that woman around," Esther said. "Didn't she pay you?"

Israel didn't reply. They watched the red end of the cigarette glow over his bruised and tired face.

"Has Dov gone to sleep?" he asked after a pause.

"No," Esther said. "He's been looking for you in every bar in town and he's really upset. He didn't even eat his supper. Has that woman paid you?"

"Of course she has," Israel said. "Women always pay what they owe."

"You said you didn't have any money."

"I don't have any change," he said. "You misunderstood me. I haven't learned Hebrew all that well yet, and I don't know if I ever will. I wasn't born here like you two. I can't fight or sing. So I have to settle for what they pay me." He removed Esther's hand gently from the steering wheel. "I have to go now. I guess Dov won't go to sleep until I return. He got used to my company during the year we've been together. Though I myself don't know why he likes me."

He started the jeep and made a U-turn on the wet sand; as he drove slowly past them, they once again saw his battered face.

"Did we offend him, Esther?" Little Dov asked.

"Don't you have other worries?"

"I don't like to hurt people's feelings, that's all," he said. "Didn't he seem offended to you?"

"No," she said.

"Good."

"It's not like you think. I don't believe it would be possible to offend him even if we wanted to."

"There's no reason to despise him."

"There's also no reason to like him," she said. "Better don't talk to me about him. He's your brother's friend. You heard what he said. Dov can't fall asleep unless he's there."

"Dov was a broken man after his wife left him. I was afraid he would do something to himself. I'm glad Israel was with him. Let's go, Esther."

"Where do you want to go?" she asked. "If you want to go swimming, we can swim right here."

"And if I don't want to go swimming?"

"Then throw them out of the house," she said. "So that we can sleep in our bed. I'm embarrassed doing it here, Dov. What if somebody sees us?"

"He'll go on his way. A man can make love to his wife anywhere he likes."

Esther sat down on the sand, bringing her long legs up and resting her chin on her knees.

"You don't like Dov, do you?" her husband asked.

"No," she said. "Neither him nor his friend. I don't know why they came here, and I don't believe they'll ever go away."

"Dov is my brother. I can't kick him out into the street."

"No," she said. "You can't do that. So maybe we should order a bed big enough for four people and sleep in it together. Or maybe big enough for five, so that when that woman comes over to see Dov, she'll fit in comfortably, too."

"What woman, Esther?"

"Just a woman," she said. "What's so strange in that? If your brother is anything like you, there's gonna be plenty of women coming to the house."

"You mean the one who's rented the jeep?"

"I know nothing about the jeep," she said. "I don't believe the jeep is what she's after. Who'd need a jeep to see a town of five thousand, which you can cover on foot in twenty minutes?"

"You shouldn't say such things, Esther," Little Dov said. "You don't know her."

"There's nothing strange in it," she said again. "Your brother is a very handsome man."

"I wouldn't know, Esther. I'm not a woman. I don't know what's so handsome about him."

"But I'm a woman. And so is she. I bet she could explain to you what's so handsome about Dov, even though he told her she looked like a whore. But that won't stop her, she'll come anyway. She'll come to him to tell him he was wrong. Dov knows how to win a woman. You have to insult her and then buy yourself a pack of cigarettes and a newspaper, lie down in bed, and wait. She'll come of her own free will to convince him he was wrong. Or right. But by then the distinction won't matter much."

Little Dov sat in silence, leaning against her knees, drawing something in the sand with a stick.

"How do you know such things, Esther?" he finally asked.

"Nobody ever told me," she said. "I just know. I feel it."

"I don't want you to feel such things, Esther."

"But I do," she said. "I can't help it. You wouldn't want me to lie, would you?"

"Try thinking of something else," he said. "And now take off your dress. You know how to make me happy."

"Why should I make you happy here?" she asked. "I have my own home and my own bed." When he didn't answer, she went on, "Oh, I forgot your brother is staying there now. But why should I do it here?"

"Because I want you to," Little Dov said. "And that should be reason enough. As long as we're together, anyway." He pushed her down on the sand and was about to pull off her dress when she jumped up and ran into the darkness, out of his reach. She burst out laughing, looking at him, and he knew he couldn't stand up because he'd look ridiculous if he did. So he stayed on his knees, his face contorted with anger, and started ripping to shreds the shirt he had been carrying.

"Too bad you're ruining that shirt," she said. "Your brother might need it. He might need it when he takes that woman to our bed."

"Esther," he said softly, "something's changed. I can feel something has changed and there's nothing I can do about it. Maybe I'm too stupid, or maybe I can't see something that's obvious to everyone else. But I don't want anything between us to change. Come here. I prefer to kill you with my own hands than to let you talk and act this way and to feel the way I'm feeling now. Yes, it'll be better if I kill you. Come here. I'll know what to do with myself afterwards." He paused and then said again, "Something's changed. Something's changed."

Suddenly he grabbed a stone from the sand and lurched after her, but she retreated quickly into the darkness; for a moment he could hear the patter of her slim bare feet on the wet, warm sand. He trudged home, all the way feeling her smell, like a dog, and following it in the dark.

ISRAEL PARKED THE JEEP WITH ITS PASSENGER SIDE wheels on the sidewalk, turned its lights off, and walked into the house. It was dark inside. Passing Dov's father's room, he stopped. He stood for a moment fingering the bones of his face and listening to the old man's deep, even breathing. Then he went into the room where he and Dov slept and saw the red glow of a cigarette end in the dark.

"You're still awake, Dov?" he asked.

"How can I sleep? I walked around the whole town asking people if they had seen you or the goddamn jeep."

"And what did they tell you?"

"That they hadn't. Maybe because they didn't know who I was looking for. Turn on the light, Israel."

"No. I've got a headache."

"Is it still so hot outdoors? I think I've sweated out all the salt I ever ate in my life."

"It's more bearable by the sea. I saw lots of people going toward the beach for an evening swim. Whole families with baby carriages."

"What time is it?"

"It's not ten yet."

Dov sat up on his makeshift bed. In a glint of light coming through the window Israel saw the drops of sweat on his forehead. There was a grimace on his face, and he was breathing heavily.

"We'll have to buy some salt pills tomorrow," Dov said. "And take them after each meal. Salt is supposed to strengthen your bones. That's what the doctors say. I'd believe them if I could find at least one who could help me. I don't believe there's one like that in the whole world. They all agree about one thing: sleeping pills are bad for you. Their like-mindedness is really praiseworthy. Haven't we got any more sleeping pills?"

"No," Israel said. "We ran out of them in Tel Aviv. You asked me that in Be'er Sheva already."

"The worst thing is that if you don't sleep for two or three nights, everybody thinks that on the fourth night you're going to sleep like a log," Dov said. "And sure enough, the fourth night you drop into a dead stupor. But what about the fifth night and the sixth? Among all those goddamned doctors, there wasn't one who knew how to help me. They give you pills that work for the first two or three nights, and then they're no good anymore. I have to lie there sweating and listen to others snore. Then I have to drink coffee throughout the day in order to stay on my feet, and at night again I can't fall asleep. At night, when you think about something, things appear much sharper and more real than by day. My old Pop can sleep easily, because he knows he's a God-fearing man and will go straight to heaven when he dies. But when I finally kick the bucket, I'll have to answer for several things. Devils will feed me sleeping pills, but those probably won't work either."

"You can't sleep because you don't really want to," Israel said. "Maybe you're afraid to sleep."

"I once fell asleep early and dreamed that I was among many people. Everyone was eating something and I was terribly hungry, so I went up to each of them in turn and asked for a bit of food, but they all refused to share with me what they had. I vividly remember approaching each and every person, but they only laughed at me. I knew that I'd die if I didn't eat something soon and I told them that, but they just kept on laughing. That's what I remember best: my terrible hunger and their laughter when I begged them for food. All the people I ever knew were there: my friends, my enemies, my brother, my mother, my father. And they all laughed at me." He paused. "That was the worst dream I ever had, Israel. And I don't know how many times more I'm going to have it. As long as I live, I guess."

"So that's why," Israel said.

"What?"

"That's why you can't sleep. You're afraid of having that dream. Don't you ever dream of your wife?"

"Yeah."

"And?"

"She's with another man," Dov said. "And I'm standing by their bed, looking at them, unable to turn away. And they laugh at me. Dina and that man. And I can't leave. I don't know why, but I can't. Something's forcing me to stand there and look at them, and listen to their laughter. I have to watch everything that man does with my Dina."

"When did you first have that dream?"

"When she first left me," Dov said. "Let's go somewhere and have a beer. I know I won't fall asleep."

"We have no money," Israel said. "We spent it all on gas and the dinner in Be'er Sheva."

"How come we have no money?" Dov asked. "Didn't you drive that tourist around all day, using up gas?"

"You didn't understand me," Israel said. "What I meant was, can we afford to waste money in bars? Think about it, Dov. One day we'll have to settle our accounts with your fat friend and pay him for the jeep. I don't think he's going to drop dead before winter."

"I can't sleep," Dov said helplessly, like a child telling his mother that he has a toothache. He lit a cigarette and Israel again saw his face: tired, mask-like, covered with sweat. "I know I won't sleep. I'll lie like this all night and listen to my brother having his way with Esther. Let's go someplace and have a beer. There isn't any left in the fridge. You deserve it. A man who has been bouncing around all day in that jeep under the scorching sun shouldn't stint himself a bottle of beer."

"Do you still think about her?" Israel asked quickly. "About Dina, your wife?"

"I already told you. Isn't that goddamn dream enough?"

"Maybe you should talk more about it and get it out of your system," Israel said. "Rich people go to doctors and tell them their dreams, and the doctors just sit there nodding their heads and then pocket their fee. Maybe it would help you."

"Days aren't so bad," Dov said, "but at night I always think about her. At night the past begins to unfold itself in my mind. I'm the only man in Israel who has his own movie theater, but it's one I can never leave. That's how I spend my nights, watching replays of the past. And the more I think about everything, the more certain I am the breakup was my fault. But that's not so bad. The worst thing is that I know that if she came back to me, I'd go on behaving exactly the same way as before. I don't even have the strength to tell myself it would be different this time. Man learns all the time and from everything, but not from love. Don't believe it if someone tells you he learned something from being in love. Maybe women can carry over the experience they amass from one affair into the next, but men don't know how to. Men are fools who want to begin everything anew with every new woman. All men. Except for me."

"You should go back to her, Dov."

"What about the bastard she's carrying?"

"You should keep that child. She's your woman. Later she'll have your kid, and the first one will stop bothering you."

"I'd have to wait," Dov said. "I'd have to wait until she gave birth to this one and then to mine. It would be a year before I'd see my kid. That year would be unbearable for both of us."

"You should go back to her," Israel said. "Sure, it'll be

hard. But you can stand a lot."

"I can't stand myself," Dov said. "And she knows that. She had enough time to get to know me well." He lay down again, resting his head on his hands. Israel couldn't see his face; the only thing he saw was a bright little star in the corner of the window. "You know, I was unfaithful to her once," Dov said. "When she went away for three days to visit her mother. I remember begging her not to go, but she had made up her mind and she was so obstinate it was like talking to a wall. And she left. In the evening when I returned home from work and opened the closet to take out a new sheet, I saw her dresses hanging there. I caught her smell and after that I just couldn't fall asleep. Finally I got up, gathered up all those dresses and piled them on the bed next to me, but that didn't help either. I lay there knowing I wouldn't sleep. So I got up again, went out, and came back with some girl I picked up in the street. And I began screwing her on top of those dresses. Then I turned on the light and saw she didn't look like my wife at all. Because, you know, somehow I had expected her to look like Dina when I turned on the light. You know, it's like when there's a kid, a little boy, who's pretending to be a girl, and everybody laughs at him and tells him he's a boy. I looked at that girl and I went mad; I started hitting her and she began to scream. People told Dina about it and that's when she left me the first time." He fell silent, and then said, "Turn on the light, Israel. We'll have lots of darkness yet. Enough to smother us."

"What happened next?" Israel asked. He was looking at the wall where he knew the light switch was. Dov didn't say anything; he continued to lie immobile, his hands behind his head. Israel, still looking in the direction of the light switch, quickly repeated his question. "What happened next, Dov?"

"You know," Dov said, as if he had not heard him, "I just remembered something. It happened before we got married. I took her to a hotel in Haifa, and afterward I lay there on the bed and watched her walk around the room. She said it was too hot for her in bed. And I saw her feet leave wet marks on the stone floor. As if she had just come out of the river. I still remember that fucking floor."

"It wasn't in Haifa," Israel said.

"No? How come?"

"You told me that story before," Israel said. "Only you said it happened in Jerusalem. I remember it well, Dov. Sometimes it seems I know your wife so well I'd be able to recognize her in the street, even if I didn't know what she looked like. I feel I know her as well as you do."

"This goddamn darkness," Dov said. He got up suddenly and started groping for the switch. "My mind gets muddled. You're right. It was in Jerusalem." He walked over to where Israel was sitting and turned on the light, saying, "Sure, in Jerusalem. I remember she was embarrassed to go to a hotel and begged me to wait, said her mother would be going away next week and we could use—Israel, what happened to your face?"

"Nothing, really," Israel said. He looked up at Dov and tried to smile. "It's still in place, isn't it?"

"Did somebody beat you up?"

"No."

Dov continued to stand by his side, staring down at him. Then he stretched out his hand and gently touched Israel's face.

"Somebody must have done it," he said softly. "And I don't need to rack my brains very hard to figure out who it was."

"No," Israel said. "A boy jumped out into the road when I was going around a bend and I had to brake hard. I was flung forward and hit my face against the steering wheel. I was all sweaty and my pants were getting stuck to the seat, so I raised myself a little, and that's when that kid jumped right in front of the jeep. I wasn't sitting properly and that's why it happened. I haven't gotten used to this heat yet, that's the trouble."

"And you never will," Dov said. "But you shouldn't lie to me."

"I'm not lying," Israel said. "Why should anybody want to hit me? I've been here only one day. Do you think that's long enough to make enemies?"

"I always make enemies," Dov said. "Sometimes all it takes is a couple of minutes. I want to know who beat you up."

"Nobody, I swear. If you intend to look for trouble, don't use me as your excuse."

"What can you swear by?"

"That won't be easy," Israel said. "I'm a Jew from Europe, so I don't really know what's holy and what's not. And I don't have any family. I could swear to you by the six million Jews who perished in the Holocaust, but I'm not sure that's something holy enough. I don't believe in God, justice, or the Day of Judgment. And I don't think people will ever improve or that they really want to. So what can I swear to you by, Dov? Maybe by those six million murdered Jews, even though all that's left of them are their ashes, and men have committed many foul deeds since. Memories don't help; they get in the way. You should know that, Dov. You can speak very beautifully of love, but I don't believe in love either. As you see, it really won't be easy for me to find something to swear to you by."

"Swear by your mother's grave," Dov said.

"No."

"Why not?"

"Because that, too, isn't something I consider holy," Israel said. "My mother was an old, stupid, and selfish woman who did everything she could to ruin my life. I never want to see her grave again. And I never feel sad when I think that she's dead. I'm sorry, Dov. Her grave isn't holy to me."

"Is there nothing in the whole world you consider holy?"

"Can there be anything holy in this world?"

"Don't answer me like a Jew," Dov said. "Jews always answer questions with questions, and that's not the best way to communicate. I'm a Jew, too, you know. I know how to play this game. But I also know that a Jew can swear only by God's Ten Commandments, and that he must cover his head when doing so. Swear by the Commandments."

"I don't believe in them," Israel said. "I guess I should have told you that earlier. There were times when men broke all the Ten Commandments one by one and nothing happened to them. And I'm sure that nothing has happened to them since and nothing ever will."

"So there's nothing you believe in?" Dov asked.

"I believe I'm going to die one day and disappear forever," Israel said. "And that that'll be my end. I can swear by that."

Dov was still standing over him and touching his face; Israel pushed his hand away.

"Do you want me to?" he asked.

"No," Dov said. "You're a strange man. You know how to squirm out of one's grasp like a snake."

"I've seen lots of people much stranger than me," Israel said. "But I don't want to think or talk about them. You can rest assured that nobody beat me up."

"Anybody who'd beat up a friend of mine would soon start regretting he was ever born," Dov said.

"I know," Israel said. "And so does everybody else in this town."

"I'm not so sure," Dov said. "There are some men here who weren't born in Israel. I'm pretty positive that if I spat one of them in the eye, he'd say it was raining."

"And if you hit him?" Israel asked.

"I'm sure he'd do nothing," Dov said. "He'd stand there waiting until I tired myself out slugging him, then he'd go to the police station and raise a racket there."

"You think none of them would defend themselves?"

"Yes, that's exactly what I think," Dov said. "I had a good look at them so I know what I'm saying."

"And how would you call them?"

"Well, how can one call them?"

"Don't answer my question with a question of your own," Israel said. "You just said you don't like that yourself."

"I'd just say I'm sorry those men didn't stay where they were born. And didn't perish there," Dov said. "You know, Israel, I don't have a very high opinion of myself. It was a shock to me when they kicked me out of the army, but it made me realize I'm not the greatest thing on earth. Still a man has got to know how to defend himself. If he doesn't, the quicker he dies, the better. For if he lives, others may die because of him. Don't you agree with that?"

"Yes," Israel said. "I agree completely. But I wouldn't have been able to put it that simply. You were born here and you were taught everything in a very straightforward manner: this is bad, this is good. I was taught differently: this is very bad for some, but good for others. Actually my teachers taught me nothing that could be useful to me here." He got up from his chair, walked over to the mirror, and peered at his face. "Yes, they taught me nothing useful," he said again.

There was a knock at the front door and Dov moved back to his makeshift bed.

"It's probably that guy from the airport I promised some dough for letting me put up my notice," Dov said. "I asked him to come in the evening. Tell him I'm not here. Or that I'm asleep and you don't want to wake me up. He's probably in such a hurry to collect his money he won't want to wait until tomorrow. But tell him he has to. And tell him it'll be just as hot tomorrow as it was to-day. I'm sure he'll be glad to hear that. We shouldn't have turned the light on."

Israel opened the door. He froze in the doorway, look-ing at the woman standing in front of him, at her slender face and tired eyes. She still wore her jeans, now covered with fine red dust.

"I wanted to leave on the afternoon plane," she said, "but there was nobody here. And I couldn't leave without apologizing to you. I just couldn't." When he didn't say anything, she added, "Your house was dark all evening."

"I'm not eager to show my face. Though I don't really know why." He took a step in her direction. "So how do you like your husband's native land? Too bad you can't write him and share your impressions. Unfortunately, there is no postal service between here and there."

"I don't know what came over me," she said. "I can't understand why I did what I did. I had been standing there, watching them beating you—"

He placed his hand over her mouth.

"Shhh. I don't want Dov to find out what happened. You owe me that."

She took his hand away from her mouth, but didn't let go of it.

"Can you forgive me?" she said.

"I can do better; I can explain it all to you," he said. "What good would my forgiveness do you? Nobody has every really forgiven anybody, and yet life goes on."

"Please, forgive me," she said.

"There isn't all that much to forgive," he said. "I un-derstand why you behaved the way you did. It was be-cause your husband was a Jew and you loved him. Your tender heart made you hit me because I wouldn't defend myself. Love is by no means simple, but it'd be hard to live without it. Love justifies almost anything. It's one of man's greatest inventions."

"Don't speak that way," she said. "I don't want to understand why it happened. I want to ask your forgiveness. If I do something wrong, I want to make up for it."

"Better don't," he said. "Too many people have been hurt by good deeds and good women. Better go back to Europe tomorrow. And try to remember only the good things."

"That's what I plan to do," she said. "I'll take the morning flight to Tel Aviv and from there I'll fly to Athens. Then I'll decide what to do next." She reached into her pocket and took out some bills. "Here's your money," she said. "We both forgot about it. I owe you for the ride."

He stood still for a few seconds, then reached out his hand for the money and stuck it in his pocket.

"Yes, I can accept it now," he said. "You saw something, after all. My conscience is clean. And, as Dov said, we need the gelt."

He could feel her body moving closer to his, yet he remained still. He felt her lips on his, and then he felt her hands pulling him after her. He took a step forward and began to follow her in the direction of the light coming from the open door of the neighboring house. He stopped in the doorway to look back at the lighted window and the silhouette of a man leaning on the sill. It seemed to him he could see Dov's heavy shoulders, which were covered with sweat, even though the big man wiped them regularly with the towel that hung, gleaming whitely, over his arm. Israel stood there for a moment touching his bruised face and breathing hard. He looked at the dark mountains over the desert and at the sky over the bay; then he went in and closed the door.

HE WAS SITTING NEXT TO URSULA ON THE WARM SAND; it was noon. The beach was empty except for the two youngsters he saw descend from the plane the other day, now in their scuba gear, seeming not to mind the stifling heat.

"They look like visitors from Mars in those masks and with those air tanks on their backs," he said. "I hope they know there are sharks around here. I don't think either of them speaks Hebrew."

"Look!" she said. "It's unbelievable."

"What?"

"That old couple from the airport," she said.

He moved his head and saw the old woman leading her husband. The man was walking stiffly, playing with the microphone of his hearing aid. As before, they were both dressed in black. The only difference was that the man wore no hat today and his head had turned red from the sun; he was looking much worse than yesterday, and his eyes had sunk deeper into his skull. He said something to his wife—it seemed to them that he wanted to rest a minute—but the woman pulled him on in silence.

"Old people, when the notion gets them, there's no telling what they're gonna do," Israel said. "They were supposed to leave yesterday on the afternoon plane."

"Maybe they like it here," she said.

"Do you believe that?"

"Why not?" she asked. "Eilat is the most beautiful place I've ever visited. And it looks different every half-hour. The mountains change as the sun climbs over them. And at night it gets so dark you can't see anything three steps away."

"There isn't much to see here," he said. "They should

see Dov; then they can leave."

"There's your Dov," she said.

She pointed to the jeep coming fast along the edge of the sea; three terrified passengers clung to their seats.

"Has he gone mad?" she asked. "Why is he going so fast? Those people will go crazy with fear."

"Everybody enjoys driving fast here," Israel said. "Don't worry, no one's gonna get hurt. The worst thing that can happen to them is a spill into the bay. I think that's what Dov wants. I know him. His sense of humor is different from other people's. But you can get used to it."

"I don't think he has any sense of humor," she said, staring after the departing jeep. "It seems he doesn't like anybody and is angry at everyone."

"His wife left him," Israel said. "That's when he began acting odd. It happens to men when their women leave them. To some of them."

"It also happens to women when men leave them."

"I know," he said. "I've heard a lot of stories. All very moving. But with Dov's wife it's different. She's going to have another man's kid. And the worst thing is almost everybody knows about it and keeps reminding Dov."

"And you're the only one helping him?"

"It's he who's helping me," he said. "He's always helped me find work; this jeep was his idea, too. He brought me here. I'm staying in his brother's house."

"Yes, I know that," she said. "But that's not the problem, your living in his brother's house, is it?"

"What problem are you talking about?" he asked. "For the past few hours I thought I had no problems. Please, don't disillusion me."

"I don't think you want to live in his brother's house," she said.

"No?"

"I think you want to live in Dov's skin," she said. "You wish you were like him."

He looked at her and smiled, but his eyes didn't move.

"That's not funny," she said.

"People are always funny," Israel said. "Even if they say or do terrible things."

"I hadn't meant to offend you," she said. "And I could be wrong. But I don't think a man can change that much; I don't believe you can become a Dov. And I don't see any need for it."

"So what do you think I should do?"

She didn't answer him, only lifted her hand; he looked to where she was pointing and saw a plane coming in for a landing, its undercarriage out; then the plane flew over their heads and Israel lowered his gaze. Their eyes met.

"Why think about it?" he said.

"You don't have to think about it," she said. "Just go back to it, that's all. Try studying; it's still possible."

"Over here they don't like people who go back to Europe," Israel said. "Actually, it's more than just a question of liking. They say about them: these people are going down. And about those who come here, they say they are going up."

"And what do they say about someone who makes his living driving tourists around for a few measly pounds? Just look at him. Couldn't he be doing something else?"

Dov drove past them again and again they saw the tourists' terrified faces.

"No," Israel said. "Let Dov stay here and do whatever he wants. I can't imagine this country without him. And Dov would die if he had to go away. I'm sure of that. Just like old peasants die when they have to leave their farms and move to the city."

"Maybe you're right," she said. "Let everybody go to pot his own way. Where can I get something cold to drink?"

"There's a stand by the hotel," he said. "It's run by a

guy named Jack who speaks six languages. Unfortunately, he has nothing interesting to say in any of them. Put your sandals on: you can cut your foot on something walking barefoot."

He watched her walk away, then picked up a newspaper. A moment later someone touched his arm; he looked up.

"Israel Berg!" a man said. "Don't you recognize me?"

"Sure," Israel said. "We worked together in Herzliya. You're a bricklayer, aren't you?"

"Yes," the man said. "Now I work here. Where's Dov Ben Dov?"

"Here, in Eilat. He just drove by with some tourists. Didn't you see him?"

"No. What's new with him?"

"Nothing."

"Nothing?"

"Nothing."

"Tell him I'm here."

"I will."

"Don't forget, okay?"

"I won't."

"Do you remember my name?"

"I'll tell him I met that bricklayer from Herzliya. Dov will know who I mean. He's got a good memory."

"What makes you think he'll remember me?"

"I didn't say I thought anything."

"Why not?"

"Because thinking is my weak point," Israel said. "Look, I'd like to take a nap now."

"How can you take a nap if you're with a woman? That would be rude."

"Then I won't take a nap," Israel said.

"What's that woman like?"

"Like other women," Israel said. "Though I'm sure she thinks herself different."

"Where's she from?"

"Europe."

"You'll go to bed with her?"

"I already did."

"And how was it?"

"Great. That's why I'm so tired. I'd like to take a nap. For at least five minutes."

"I'll leave you then."

"Okay."

"You'll tell him, won't you?"

"Sure."

"You won't forget?"

"No."

"You'll tell him it was me?"

"Yes."

"Okay, I'll be going then," the man said. "Hey, I just realized something. You know what?"

"No," Israel said. "But I'm sure it must be important."

"I just realized that that woman and Dov would make a fine couple," the man said.

Israel raised himself on his elbows. "You think so?"

"Yes," the man said. "Dov is a big man, and she's rather petite. They would look nice together. My mother was also shorter than my father, and my sister is much shorter than my brother-in-law. Has Dov seen her?"

"Yes."

"And? What did he say?"

"He told her his name and that was it. You must have forgotten that Dov has a wife."

"Had a wife."

"Dov still has a wife," Israel said. "And she'll come back to him when he wants her to. He won't even have to whistle to make her come running. It'll be enough if he just thinks to himself that he wants her back; she'll know."

"How come you're so irritable? A young man like you? Well, I'll be going now. Just tell Dov I'm here, okay?"

"I will," Israel said.

Israel did not look again at the man who stood before him hoping their conversation would continue; instead, he looked toward the hotel where he could see Ursula walking back in his direction, then he moved his gaze to where the jeep was and saw Dov drinking a bottle of beer. Finally, the man left; Israel placed a newspaper over his face and lay down on the sand. He heard Ursula approach and sit down next to him.

"Are you asleep?" she asked him softly.

"No," he said. "I'm thinking. I'm thinking about leaving Israel and getting back to studying planes. It won't be easy for me to leave. I'm trying to imagine Dov's reaction. We've been together a long time."

"He can't stop you," she said. "He'll just have to accept your decision."

"And if he doesn't?"

"He'll have only himself to blame."

"Dov can't understand why his wife left him," Israel said. "He spends a lot of time mulling over it, but I know he'll never find the answer. Is he really to blame himself for that?"

She looked at him, at his slim body and handsome, alert face, then turned her head away.

"So it's like I thought after all," she said. "You want to be like him. Like Dov Ben Dov. Maybe with time you'll manage to adopt or emulate all his good points and virtues. But you'll never have his vices. And you'll have only yourself to blame for that." She stood up and held out her hand to him. "Come, let's go have some coffee."

They left the beach and started walking toward town. They stopped at the nearest café. Ursula sat down at an outdoor table and Israel went inside. There was nobody there; a red beaded curtain hung stiffly at the end of the room.

"Does anybody run this place?" Israel asked loudly after standing by the bar for a while.

The red curtain swung open and a portly man stepped behind the bar. He placed his elbows on it and looked at Israel.

"I run it," he said.

"You don't run it well," Israel said. "You should stand behind the bar and wait for customers. Give me two coffees."

"There's no coffee here," the man said.

"What do you mean?" Israel asked. "Your coffee-maker is hot."

"You're mistaken."

Israel touched the espresso. "It's hot," he said.

"You're that friend of Ben Dov's?"

"Yes."

"I don't want you to drink coffee in my place," the man said.

"Why?"

"That's my business. Just like this place is mine. Don't you understand Hebrew, mister? How long have you been in this country?"

Israel didn't answer.

"I want to know why you won't sell me coffee," he finally said. "You don't think you can insult me for no reason, do you?"

The man began to walk away, but then came back and faced Israel. He was heavy, fat, and white, as if the sun beating down on everything for fourteen hours a day had never touched his skin.

"I don't like your type," the man said. "Does that satisfy you?"

"No."

"I was with Abraham Stern. Do you at least know who that was?"

"Sure."

"No, you don't," the man said. "He was a man who wanted to fight. Who waited all by himself on the rooftop while police surrounded the house." He paused and then said, "There was no way they could have gotten him alive."

"I don't see what this has to do with my coffee," Israel said. "Everybody in this country knows that Stern was a hero."

"But there is no street named after him," the man said. "What happened to your face?"

"Is that what's bothering you?"

"Not only that. Don't ever come here again. Neither you nor Ben Dov. I don't want any brawls in my place."

"Should I tell him that?"

"Why ask? Don't you tell him everything? You tell him to settle your scores for you, don't you? But I don't like it when a Jew is hit in the face and he won't defend himself. It reminds me of something I left behind. Something I don't want to go back to. You can tell him all that. I'm not afraid of him. I was never afraid of anything or anybody."

"Did many people see me yesterday on the beach?" Israel asked quietly.

"Some," the man said. "And everybody will tell you the same thing. I'm sorry, but I can't help you."

"No," Israel said. "You're not sorry at all."

"All right, I'm not. Now go away."

"Okay," Israel said. "But you can at least do one thing for me. Tell me who spread the story around."

"Do you know the name of the prettiest girl in town?"

"No."

"Then ask your friend's brother," the man said. "He'll know. He married her. Now go away."

Israel went out into the sun and stepped up to Ursula,

a smile on his face. She didn't see him; she was looking toward the bay and the white houses of Aqaba.

"Ursula," he said, "we won't get any coffee in this bar. But I have some news for you. I've decided to leave on the earliest plane possible."

"What happened?"

"Nothing," he said. "Nothing happened. But the owner of this bar convinced me I ought to study. There are many things in life I still know nothing about. And I should."

"Tell me what happened," she said. "Something must have happened if even a fool like me can feel it."

"It's a long story," he said. "My head begins to spin when I think about it. Dov lost his wits when his wife left him and he started getting into trouble. The last time it happened, in Tel Aviv, we decided I'd take the blame, because otherwise they'd have put him away for a few years."

"What kind of trouble?"

"That word isn't very precise, you're right," Israel said. "Well, to start, Dov came home one day and found his wife with a man. He later told the court he had to defend himself because the man attacked him."

"What happened to the man?"

"I don't know," he said. "Whatever it is that happens to people after death. There are many theories. Anyway, that last time in Tel Aviv, I told the judge I was the guilty one, but he didn't really believe me. He gave me a suspended sentence and once again warned Dov. And so we came here, where Dov's brother is a fisherman, and things got complicated again. Dov's brother has competition: three guys who fish from motorboats and make ten times more money than he does. So when Dov arrived in Eilat, his brother expected Dov to help him. But Dov's got to keep out of trouble."

"So that's why you didn't defend yourself yesterday?"

"Yes," he said. "I couldn't."

"Does Dov know about it?"

"No. I was afraid he'd want to settle the matter in his own way. And that would have been very bad."

"So he is the strong one and you're the weak one? And when they beat you up, he can't know? Is that it?"

"Yes," he said. "You got it. Let's go, now. I don't want everybody to hear us."

"It's only six," she said.

"Go back home. I'll come over later. I want to talk to Dov first."

She rose from the table and left; he watched her until she disappeared around the corner, then he went back inside.

"What do you want?" the owner asked, getting up and moving in his direction. "Didn't I tell you not to show your mug around here again?"

Israel didn't answer; he took off his sunglasses and slipped them into his pocket. Then he picked up from the floor a heavy, iron-legged chair and smashed it into the coffee-maker, jumping away from the clouds of steam.

"I just wanted to tell you that you were right," he said. "There's no coffee in your place." He threw the chair on the floor and walked out into the street.

THE TWO YOUNG, SUNTANNED COPS SAT HEAVILY IN their chairs, their elbows propped on the table, their caps in front of them. It was past sunset, but the heat still hung heavily in the air; the scorched earth resisted the wind, which was slowly coming to life over the bay—its soft rustle could be heard now and then through the agonizing clatter of the electric fan.

"Would you like some coffee?" Dov asked.

"In Eilat nobody can live without coffee," one of the cops said. "You'll find that out if you stay here longer."

"How long do you plan to stay, Dov?" the other cop asked.

"Why do you ask?" Dov said. "Are you going to write down my answers?"

"We're off duty," the cop said, indicating his cap lying on the table. "You've met cops before, haven't you?"

"Right," Dov said. "I'll tell my sister-in-law to make us some coffee."

He went to the kitchen. One of the cops got up with an effort and stepped up to the wall.

"Me and the younger Dov were in the army together," he said.

"You never told me you were a paratrooper," the second cop said.

"Didn't I?"

"No."

"Well, now you know. And let me tell you, I didn't enjoy all that parachute jumping one bit. The last jump was as scary as the first, even though our instructors claimed we'd get used to it. I never did. And I'm sure he didn't either." He returned to his chair, again propped his bronzed elbows on the table, and leaned his chin on his fists. "You should tell us why you did it," he said to Israel. "That was a foolish thing to do, you know."

"I already told you."

"No, you didn't."

"The coffee-maker was rusty," Israel said.

"What a strange guy," the cop said, turning to his partner. "He keeps answering me like he's Dov Ben Dov." He looked at Israel. "But he'll never be Ben Dov, right?"

"Right," the second cop said. "He's not Ben Dov's size."

"You should think it over," the first cop said. "If you apologize to the owner and agree to pay for the damage, he may withdraw his complaint."

"And if he doesn't?"

"The case will go to court."

"And how much am I gonna get?" Israel asked. "Is there a special law against smashing coffee-makers? What's the usual sentence? Getting shot seven times in the ass with sour milk? Will you two be part of the execution squad?"

Dov came into the room and placed two cups and a coffeepot in front of the cops.

"I'll get myself a chair and be right back," he said.

"These two will be free in a moment," said the first cop. He gestured at Israel. "Dov, you should explain to your friend that it'd be better if he apologized to that chap. And you should tell him he's himself, not you. It's time he knew that." He got up and put on his cap. "We'll be going now," he said.

"You wanted coffee, didn't you?" Dov said.

"Your friend is doing his best to insult us," the cop said. "It'll be better if we go. He has no right to act this way, Dov."

"Have a cup," Dov said.

"No. Your friend is making fools of us."

Dov walked them to the door and stood there for a moment until he heard the engine of their car start; then he returned to the room.

"Why didn't you tell me anything?"

"There was no time," Israel said.

"How much time does one need to say he had a row in a bar?"

"We weren't alone."

"We were sitting here alone for an hour before those cops arrived."

"No," Israel said. "We weren't alone. Your brother's wife is always listening at the door. She is also listening to what we are saying now. We haven't been alone for one minute."

"You won't tell me why you smashed that coffee-maker?"

"It's not worth talking about," Israel said. "Isn't that so, Esther?"

They watched the door open slowly; Esther entered the room, not in the least embarrassed.

"Yes," she said. "Neither you nor that coffee-maker are worth talking about."

Dov stepped up to her, gripped her by the arm, and forced her to look at him. "How old are you, Esther?" he asked.

"I'm not twenty yet," she said, looking at Dov's hand tightening on her arm.

"Isn't it enough that you're a whore?" he said. "Do you have to be a snoop too?" He pushed her against the wall. "What have you got to tell me, Esther?"

"She has already told everybody," Israel said. "You're the only person she hasn't told the story to yet."

"Esther," Dov said, "my brother will be back in an hour. When he arrives I'll say good-bye to him, then Israel and I will leave. But for that one hour, we want to be alone. Is that too much to ask?"

"No one said you had to leave," Esther said.

"Is that too much to ask, Esther?"

"No one said you had to leave," she said again. "This is your brother's house."

"No, I don't think she wants to kick you out," Israel said. "She isn't a bad kid. Maybe she's just too much like you. But she loves your brother and knows that he loves you. You shouldn't be so rough on her. She didn't ask you to leave."

"No," Dov said. "Not yet. But I'm old, Israel. For someone who's forty, getting kicked out into the street is no laughing matter, believe me."

"Where will you go?" Esther asked. "As long as you let Israel tag along, you'll be a laughingstock no matter where you go." She turned in Israel's direction. "He allows people to hit him in the face." She moved a step closer to Israel. "Why don't you tell him?" she asked. "Why do you lie to him? You can tell him the truth."

"You'll do it better," Israel said. "So you tell him. Just like you told everybody else." Suddenly he got up and walked over to the window. "You're a clever girl, Esther. And you know so much. You know that some men beat me up on the beach yesterday, and you know I didn't want to tell Dov about it. And you know the reason I didn't; you know the situation he's in. And you know many other things. Except one. The one which is most important. And until you find that out, you won't have a moment's rest. That's why I can't hate you, Esther. You're innocent because you don't know the most important thing."

"What is it I don't know?"

"You don't know what I'm talking about," Israel said. "You don't know what's making you restless. You can feel something is happening to you, but you don't know what it is. I do."

"But you're too big a coward to tell me, aren't you?"

"No," Israel said. "I simply intend to wait until others do it for me. I'm paying you back in kind."

"Didn't I tell you to leave this room, Esther?" Dov

asked. "Do you want me to put it more strongly?"

She didn't budge. She kept staring at Israel, and they both saw that her lips were moving soundlessly.

"Then let me tell you something," she finally said. "I'll tell you what's most important."

"You can't," Israel said. "You don't know."

"I do," she said. "And it won't take long. It's much simpler than you think."

"Yes," Israel said. "It's much simpler than either of us thinks. But you don't know what it is."

Little Dov came in, but Esther still didn't move. She stood in the middle of the room, leaning slightly forward and looking at Israel.

"I'm famished, Esther," Little Dov said. "I barely had any breakfast."

"You don't look well," Israel said. "You looked much better when you were in the army." He pointed at Little Dov's picture hanging on the wall. "Didn't he, Esther?"

"Esther, I'm hungry," Little Dov said. He walked up to his wife and touched her arm, but she pushed him away violently.

"Hey, Esther, what's wrong?" Little Dov asked. "Why are you so pale?"

"It concerns you and that woman," Esther said to Israel, as if her husband had not spoken at all. "You don't think she's after you, do you? You're not that stupid. She's after Dov. She wants to get into his bed through yours. Because she knows that that's the only way to catch his interest. She knows that well. As well as I do. Was that the important thing you wanted to tell me?"

"No," Israel said. "That wasn't it."

"I think it was," Esther said. "Your spending last night with her doesn't mean a thing. She went to bed with you out of pity. She saw you get beat up. And then she hit you in the face herself. Women often go to bed with men out of pity. I should know. I did it many times."

"But Esther," Little Dov said, "You told me—You swore to me—" He suddenly looked much younger than ever before; he walked up to her quietly, as if afraid of the sound of his own footsteps. "No, Esther. That can't be true. You swore to me!"

"Don't touch me," she said. "You're as big a fool as he is. Okay, I swore to you. So what? For three days each month any woman can swear she's a virgin if she's with as big a fool as you or him. Some women can even do it for four or five days."

"But you swore to me!"

"No," she said. "I'm a woman. I'm forbidden to swear. I'm unclean."

"But you did!"

"So what?" she said. "Ask that woman what she told Israel when she went to bed with him." She took a step forward; she and Israel were now face to face. "I also told men many things before I met my husband," she said. "I started screwing around when I was fourteen and didn't really know what sex was. Do you believe me now?"

"You still haven't said what's most important," Israel said. "You haven't said it."

"No?"

"No," he said. "I'm sorry, Esther, but that's not all."

Their eyes followed her as she walked out into the hall and opened the door to the father's room.

"Pop," she said, "please come out for a moment." She waited, leaning against the doorjamb, but he didn't answer. "You told me you loved me like your own daughter," she went on. "And you told me to— Don't you want me to give you a grandchild anymore?"

Finally the old man appeared. He stopped in the doorway, facing them; Esther placed her arm around him.

"Pop, look at Israel, please," she said. "Can that man be better than Dov?"

"Is that so hard?" the old Dov asked.

"You don't understand, Pop," Esther said. "The thing is, there's this woman who—" Suddenly she fell silent and looked at them helplessly, as if she had forgotten what she wanted to say.

"Why do you ask me?" the old man said. "You're a woman yourself. You're unclean. You should know what a woman would do if she could choose."

"She doesn't know," Israel said. "That's the whole problem; she doesn't know."

"You really think you are better than my son Dov?" the old man asked Israel. "If so, I envy you."

"Take her away from here," Dov said to his brother. "She's ill." He stepped up to her and touched her forehead; then he walked over to his father. "It's a pity one can't choose one's parents," he said. "Now get out." And when the old man didn't move, he gave him a shove and closed the door behind him.

"Do you believe me now?" Esther asked softly.

"Take her away," Dov said to his brother. "I'll leave either tonight or tomorrow. But now just take her away." He tossed him his car keys. "Right now."

"Where should I take her?" Little Dov asked.

"She's your wife," Dov said. "I don't know. Why ask me?" He slammed the door behind them and sat down at the table. "She's ill. I'm sorry."

"She's innocent," Israel said. "She spoke the truth. Is it her fault she realized something we didn't?" He went up to the window and raised the curtain. "See that light? Ursula is waiting."

"So?"

"She's waiting for you."

"Don't you start that, too!"

"No," Israel said. "I'm not starting anything. I've finished with her. Now it's your turn." He let the curtain fall. "But let's wait some more. Or rather, let her wait." He took a chair, turned it around, and sat down facing Dov.

"Did I ever tell you about my brother?"

"No. I didn't know you had a brother," Dov said.

"He's dead now," Israel said. "He was in Britain during the war. When he came back to Poland, the Commies arrested him and sentenced him to death. He spent seven years in prison awaiting execution. Then they let him out."

"They did?"

"Yes," Israel said. "They let him out, but he never left that prison. He stayed in it forever."

"What are you talking about, man?"

"I can talk about anything you like," Israel said. "Somebody who was once in Madrid told me that the hearses there are painted white and look like a cross between an ice cream cart and a jukebox. Want me to tell you more about it?"

"Why don't you just go to sleep?" Dov said. "You've had enough for today. So have I."

"Of course I'll go to sleep," Israel said. "But what about you?"

"What about me?"

"Will you fall asleep? Will you?"

"What are you driving at?"

"Maybe you'll dream of your wife again," Israel said. "Maybe you'll wake up in the middle of the night and start feeling scared that you won't fall asleep again and then you really won't, until dawn."

"What are you driving at?" Dov asked again.

"You know," Israel said, "my brother had a wife he brought over from Ireland. And when he was finally released from prison, he told me he dreamed the same dream over and over again. He was driving with his wife through a strange city, and he left her in the car for a minute and went to get something; when he returned, he couldn't find either her or the car. So he began searching all over the city, asking everybody he met if they had seen his wife or his car, but no one understood what he was saying. And those who did laughed at him."

"They laughed at him?"

"Yes," Israel said. "Just like in that dream you had. Remember that dream where you were hungry and no one would share his food with you? That's the same kind of dream. My brother had it for seven years."

"And what happened to him?" Dov asked.

"Exactly what you think. Yes, exactly that. Two years after his release from prison."

"I don't believe you," Dov said.

"Why?"

"You read this story somewhere. Or somebody told you."

"No," Israel said. "It's true. He did what you think he did when he came out of prison and realized she wouldn't come back to him. He didn't blame her. After all, he had been sentenced to death."

"Why are you telling me all this?" Dov asked. "I know you. You haven't told me yet what's really on your mind. Can't you say it outright?"

"I'm worried about you," Israel said. "That's all."

"Many people have worried about me," Dov said. "But so far nothing's happened."

"You've killed a man," Israel said. "Is that nothing?"

"You know why I did it."

"I know much more," Israel said. "I know that one day you're going to kill yourself. That's why I'm telling you all this. One night when you won't be able to fall asleep you'll suddenly realize that you should have done it long ago. And then you'll be in such a hurry to do it you won't have time to think it over." He got up and went to the window. They hadn't turned on the light; he lifted the curtain and stood bathed in the weak glow coming from the window on the opposite side of the yard. "She's still waiting," he said. "Isn't it awful?"

"What?" Dov asked.

"That people learn from others things they should know themselves. Take Esther. Or Ursula. Or me, or you."

"What do you want from me?" Dov asked. He spoke softly, looking very tired; Israel could barely see his face in the light falling past his shoulder. "Do you want me to get into new trouble?"

"That woman will give you sleep," Israel said.

"No. Just because you liked it with her doesn't mean I'll like it too. I've tried going to bed with other women but it never was the same. Never."

"I thought about it last night," Israel said. "I switched on the light and watched her go to the bathroom. And I saw her feet leave wet marks on the tiles. It made me think of Dina, your wife. And of you. I thought of you lying here in the dark trying to fall asleep. And I knew you'd stay awake until morning. Wasn't I right?"

Dov got up. He walked to the window and tugged the curtain down. Israel saw his face up close: it was pale and weary, a mask.

"Yes," Dov said.

"Go to her," Israel said. "She's waiting for you."

"I haven't stood trial for rape yet," Dov said. "And I don't intend to."

"What do you mean, rape?" Israel said. "Everybody knows she's after you. Esther. Your old dad. Your brother."

"And you too?"

"And me too," Israel said.

"No," Dov said, "I can't do that. I don't know why but I can't."

"You're afraid of her," Israel said. "You're not afraid that you won't enjoy fucking her but that she won't enjoy being fucked by you. Is that right?"

"You're a bastard," Dov said. "A stupid bastard with a big mouth. Why do I take such a bastard with me everywhere I go?"

"Because you're a pal," Israel said. "There are guys who'd slug me for telling them the truth."

"Remember it was you who said she was after me; I didn't," Dov said. He grabbed his shirt from the back of a chair and went out.

"Not only me," Israel said. "Everybody did."

He went to the corner where their canvas bag stood and rummaged in it until he found a small vial of sleeping pills. He took out two pills, threw the bag back in the corner, and went to the kitchen to get some water. When he returned, he stopped for a moment by the window, staring toward the light coming from the other house; then he pulled the curtain back in place. It was quiet; he turned off the fan and lay down. He could hear the wind blowing from the bay and traveling over the dark landscape in the direction of the mountain range and on toward the desert where everything was bright and distinct in the moonlight.

DOV CROSSED THE DARK YARD AND WALKED INTO THE house. He leaned against the doorjamb of Ursula's room and stood there, staring at her sitting on the bed; she turned her head away when she saw him and didn't look at him again.

"You're surprised, aren't you?" she asked, finally.

"I don't know," he said.

"Yes," she said, turning her slim, weary face in his direction. "I can tell you're surprised. You're surprised that I'm not surprised. Aren't you? But it's not as complicated as you may think. Israel told me he'd come at eight. By the time it was half past eight, I was pretty sure that it would be you who would come, not him. It's past eleven now. I've been expecting you for three hours."

"I can leave," he said. "I can leave at once."

"Do you really believe that?"

"I believe everything I hear about a woman," Dov said. "And everything a woman tells me."

"No," she said. "Don't leave yet. Don't leave until you tell me why you came."

"Do I have to tell you that?"

"You must have been thinking something while crossing the yard," she said. "Don't you have enough courage to tell me what it was?"

"It didn't take me long to cross it," he said. He opened the front door and pointed toward his brother's dark house. "See? It's just a few steps."

"Then you must have been thinking something earlier," she said. "Close the door and tell me why you came."

He stood in the doorway, motionless, continuing to look at the woman sitting on her bed three yards away from him, a book by her side.

"Did anybody tell you I was waiting for you?" she asked. "Or did I myself suggest it to you in any way?"

"I'm going," he said. "It's enough that I made a fool of myself."

"You won't stop being a fool just by closing the door," she said. "You'll go on being one as long as you believe it was you I was waiting for. It wasn't. I'm sorry, but that's the truth."

"I'm sorry, too," he said.

"I sat here and waited for Israel," she said. "And I think I know what happened. Everybody thought it was you I was after, didn't they?"

"I didn't," he said.

"But you changed your mind?"

"I don't know," he said. "Maybe I didn't. Maybe I came here only because that's what everybody was telling me to do all evening. I don't know."

"But I do," she said. "I'm very sorry, but it's not you I wanted to come here; it was Israel."

"He'll come," he said.

"But you'll go on thinking I wanted you," she said. "And so will he, because he considers himself a lesser and weaker man. And everybody else thinks that way too. You'll feel very foolish now, going away and telling them you didn't go to bed with me, won't you?"

"I don't know," he said. "Maybe."

"You have nothing to worry about," she said. "Nobody will believe you if you say you didn't sleep with me. They'll think you are protecting Israel and you'll only gain in their eyes. They'll think even more highly of you and hold him in even greater contempt. Whatever you do it works in your favor. Just think of it: a man screws a woman his friend might be in love with, but he claims he didn't do it so that his friend won't look ridiculous. Isn't that generous of him?"

"Yes," he said. "Can I leave now?"

"You can," she said. "But you won't. You are afraid to leave too soon. Somebody might see you, and your reputation would be spoiled forever. Good night."

"Leave Eilat," he said. "Take the first plane tomorrow and leave. That'll be best for all of us."

"Not for all of us. Only for you. When I leave, people will say that that whore was ashamed of spending one night with Israel and the next with Dov, so she left. So this, too, would work out to your advantage."

"Leave anyway," he said.

"I will. If Israel leaves with me," she said.

"Why should he leave with you?"

"And why should he stay?"

"His place is here," Dov said. "What guarantee can you give him that nobody will insult him? Can you guarantee that when he goes to Europe with you nobody there will tell him he doesn't belong?"

"No," she said. "I can't guarantee that. If somebody insults him, he'll have to take care of that himself. It'll be his responsibility and his risk. Over here he'll always be under your protection. That's why it's better for him to leave. Good night."

He didn't move.

"I said good night."

"Will you leave Eilat?"

"Good night. I've told you good night three times already. Why are you still here? Are you afraid to go out? You've been here for fifteen minutes. That's long enough to screw a woman. You can go away now. I want to undress and go to sleep."

"You really want him to leave with you?"

"Yes. And he will," she said. "You can ask him yourself. I'm going to sleep now. You should too. I'm sorry I have to disrobe in your presence, but there's no reason for me to sleep in my dress. So now I'll take it off and then climb into bed, and nothing—I repeat, nothing—is going to happen between us."

He watched her take off her dress and throw it on a chair, then walk naked across the room to the mirror and begin brushing her hair; he looked at her and at the wet footprints she left on the tiles. Then she lay down on the bed and covered herself with a sheet, but only up to her middle.

"You see?" she said. "Nothing's happened. Do you still believe you're better than he is?"

"No, I don't," he said. "The worst thing is that tomorrow we'll have to face each other again and go on with our lives."

"Remember one thing: everybody has to live his own life," she said. "You can fight for two, even make love for two, but nobody's strong enough to feel shame for two. Actually, nobody's strong enough to really feel shame. Good night. Tomorrow you can tell them all I was a lousy lay. That's what men always say about women they didn't have."

She turned off the light; he stood a moment longer looking at the stone tiles until her wet footprints faded slowly away in front of his eyes. Then he closed the door and left.

She was sitting in a café waiting for Israel. She had drunk a cup of coffee and was trying to order a snack from the menu, but she had trouble communicating with the waiter; he was a Jew from one of the Arab countries and his Hebrew was even worse than hers.

"I've been here just three years," he said.

"And you haven't learned to read yet?" she asked.

"I've been here just three years," he said with complete indifference, which—as she knew—was meant to mask his astonishment at her stupidity.

"Does anybody here speak German?" she asked loudly, turning toward the only other client: a man who was sitting by himself with a bottle of beer and reading a newspaper.

"Yes. Can I help you?" he asked.

"I'd like to order a sandwich," she said. "That's all. But he's been here just three years."

The man said something to the waiter, then took his bottle of beer and moved over to her table. He looked very tired, and it was impossible to tell his age.

"You're from Hamburg, aren't you?"

"Yes," she said. "Can you tell by my accent?"

"I can," he said. "I was born in Berlin."

"And how long have you been here?"

"Twenty-eight years," he said. "That's longer than you're alive."

"Berliners have always been the nicest Germans," she said. "That's what everybody says. You know, my father-in-law is from Berlin, too. And he's the nicest man in the world."

"Yes," he said. "People from Berlin are the nicest." He smacked the newspaper that was lying on his knees. "But now the Germans are putting up walls. And soon they'll start shooting children again. Have you read about it?"

"My father-in-law is the nicest man in the world," she said quickly. "You know, he's been continuously drunk for forty years and my mother-in-law hasn't noticed anything. That's quite an achievement, don't you think?"

"He'd stop drinking here," the man said, turning his face to her. "Especially if he was an insurance agent like I am. Today I spent ten hours walking around in the heat and I haven't earned enough to pay for a bottle of beer."

"Don't people want to buy insurance?"

"What should they insure themselves against?" he asked. "Against themselves? Many former criminals live here. I'll give you an example: there are three new fishermen here who have motorboats. I told them to insure the boats and they said, Look, we're the biggest thieves around here. If we don't steal them, nobody will. They're forgetting that nobody has to steal their boats. It's enough to put some sand in their engines to ruin them forever. Anybody can do it. Especially at night; nobody guards those boats. My God."

The waiter brought a cup of coffee and a plate with a piece of bread with a slice of meat.

"You didn't order coffee, did you?" the insurance agent asked.

"Never mind," she said. "I'll drink it. The waiter has been here for just three years."

"It's not healthy to drink so much coffee," he said. "But here in Israel, one simply has to."

"Oh, I like being reckless," she said. "Same as those men who own the motorboats. Pass me the sugar, please." He handed her the sugar bowl and she heaped two spoonfuls into her cup and then added a third one. "I like my coffee very sweet," she said. "How does that German saying about coffee go?"

"Coffee should be dark as night, sweet as sin, and

strong as love," he said. His tired face twisted into a gloomy smile. "Funny it's the Germans who say that. Germans don't know anything about coffee."

Israel entered the café and came over to their table; seeing him, the insurance agent said good-bye and left.

"What did he want?" Israel asked.

"Nothing," she said. "But if I had wanted to buy insurance, he could have sold it to me. He's from Berlin, and I asked if anybody spoke German. Do you have your passport?"

"You still want me to go away with you?"

"Has anything changed?"

"No," he said. "Nothing has changed. And nothing will. I can't go with you."

"Is it because of something Dov said?"

"No," he said. "It's because of what everybody will say. When an American goes to Paris and stays there for thirty years, drinking himself blind and telling everybody he doesn't like America, everybody considers him a charming eccentric for as long as his money lasts. But if a Jew goes somewhere, everybody begins to act surprised. Nobody really knows why it's so. But that's the way it's always been."

"It's exactly the same thing Dov told me yesterday when he got his doors mixed up."

"If two people say the same thing, it means there's something to it," he said. "But it's not only the two of us who think this way."

"You're wrong," she said. "People can live wherever they want as long as they have money or work. It's not like you say. You just lack the strength to leave Dov and start leading your own life."

"Maybe," he said. "Words don't mean much. Look, stay here as long as you want. And come again as soon as you can. Nothing will change during your absence."

The waiter placed a cup of coffee in front of Israel.

"It'll change," she said. She gazed for a moment at the next table, where the insurance agent had left his newspaper on the way out; then she picked up the sugar bowl. "How much sugar do you take?" she asked.

"None," he said.

"Take some," she said. She put one and then another spoon into his cup. "Things change," she said.

"I have to go," he said. "Dov has been showing tourists around all day, but some want to see King Solomon's mines by night, in artificial light, although you'd think that after all those hours in the sun they'd have enough light until the next day. So I have to drive them there."

"Will you come over tonight?"

"Yes," he said. "As soon as I take those tourists back to their hotel."

"What time?"

"I don't know," he said. "I don't know when they'll have enough. They might not like the mines at all. They might sleep throughout the trip and I may have to talk aloud to myself to stay awake."

He got up.

"So you don't want to go away with me?" she asked.

"You wouldn't believe me if I said I didn't," he said. "The truth is I simply don't think it's possible for me to leave."

"You're afraid to leave Dov alone?"

"Nothing will happen to him as long as he doesn't beat up somebody," he said. "But all he needs to start a fight is some excuse. He's got reasons enough."

He went out and walked up to the jeep parked by the curb. Dov was leaning against the hood, drinking beer straight from the bottle.

"Where are those guests?" Israel asked.

"In the Eilat Hotel," Dov said. "The man's name is Borgenicht." He took the car keys out of his pocket and tossed them to Israel.

"I'll drive you home," Israel said.

"Did I say I wanted to go home? I'm not going back there until they all go to sleep. My father, my brother, Esther. Want some beer?"

"Yes."

Dov passed him the bottle.

"I'll get drunk today," Dov said.

"You'll feel dreadful tomorrow."

"Tomorrow? I feel dreadful today. I've been feeling dreadful half my life, and a bottle of brandy is only eight pounds."

"Wait for me," Israel said. "We'll get drunk together. That'll cost us sixteen pounds."

"No," Dov said. "Spend the night with your girl. You got me into an awful fix yesterday."

"They got me into an awful fix," Israel said. "Your father, your brother. And Esther."

"Esther is a big, foolish child," Dov said. "You shouldn't listen to her gibberish."

Israel smiled. "Dov."

"Yes?"

"Don't you really understand anything? Do I have to open your eyes for you every time?"

"Don't," Dov said. "I beg you, don't explain anything to me. You told me yesterday what I was supposed to do and I've never felt as bad as today. Don't tell me anything more. There's nothing you could say in the whole world that would interest me. Is there any beer left?"

"Some."

"Let me have it."

Israel returned the bottle to him.

"I won't stand it here much longer," Dov said. "I have to leave."

"We'll both leave."

"But each of us will go his own way."

"That'll happen only if you want it to happen," Israel

said. "Otherwise I'll stick with you."

"Don't you want to go to Europe anymore?" Dov asked. "Don't you want to start a new life?"

"No," Israel said. "I have to let this one run its course first."

Dov didn't say anything; he threw the bottle into the dark and must have hit someone with it, because they heard a curse.

"You're still young," he finally said. "Maybe elsewhere you could lead a better life. I don't know. I can't advise you. It could work both ways, you know. I can't say. I've never been to Europe."

"I'm a Jew," Israel said. "That's what they ask you about first, and only then about your age. I was in Europe, so I know."

"What do you want to do?"

"Nothing. I'll stay here. We both will."

"I want to go away," Dov said. "I'm fed up with Eilat. I'm fed up with my father, my brother, his crazy wife. I want to get drunk."

"Wait for me," Israel said. "We'll get drunk together."

"What about Ursula?"

"I don't know. Maybe she'll get drunk with us."

"If I had the money, I'd get this whole town drunk," Dov said. "The whole goddamn town together, the rabbis, the mayor, and the three hundred miners working in King Solomon's mine. And all those fucking tourists who come here and pretend they like my country, I'd get them drunk, too. So they'd all feel awful tomorrow. The way I do today. I slept three hours last night, that's it. And tonight I won't sleep any more than that. I'll get this whole goddamn town drunk, and then we'll go away."

"Where to?"

"I don't know yet," Dov Ben Dov said. "I haven't thought about it. We'll decide on the way."

HE WAS WALKING DOWN THE LONG HOSPITAL HALL WITH the doctor, a young blond man with a heavily tanned face. It was six in the evening.

"Don't you have anything that makes a man full of pep after he has drunk too much and slept too little?" Dov asked.

"No," the doctor said. "If I did, I'd take it myself. So, what happened last night?"

"I don't know," Dov said. "We went to a bar—my friend, his girlfriend, and I. We had a few drinks and then she left, saying she was sleepy, and we stayed on and drank some more. Then my friend said to me: Let's leave the jeep here and walk home. If a cop stops us for drunk driving, we'll be in big trouble. So we walked home and went to bed. I fell asleep almost immediately and slept for about two hours when some men came to our house to tell me my brother had been beaten up by some fishermen and taken to the hospital. After that I slept maybe another three hours."

"Do you know why they beat him up?"

"No, I don't," Dov said. "Maybe he started the fight himself. There's been a lot of bad blood between them. Actually I had been thinking it wouldn't be too bad if one of them gave him a good licking; it might be a lesson to him."

The doctor didn't say anything. Dov looked at him.

"Hey," he said, stopping and taking the doctor by the arm. "It's nothing serious, is it?"

The doctor gently disengaged himself. "He's in here," he said. "Be nice to him."

"Is it serious?"

"Be nice to him," the doctor said again. "And then

come to see me."

He gave him a gentle shove and Dov walked into the room. Little Dov had the room to himself; Dov approached his bed.

"Hi, Dov," Little Dov said. "Why didn't Esther come with you?"

"I don't know." Dov said. "Somebody from the hospital dropped in and asked the old man to visit you. But he wouldn't because today is Friday. So I came instead."

"I don't feel well."

"What's wrong with you?"

"I don't know. Ask one of those white coats. I got slugged a few times and I lost consciousness."

"Was it those fishermen who fixed you like that? What made you pick a fight with them?"

"I didn't, Dov. I was walking along the beach, sometime around six, not even looking where I was going, when suddenly these three guys jumped me and started pummeling away. I began defending myself and threw a few good punches before one of them whacked me on the head from behind and I just folded up and went to sleep."

"Why did they attack you?"

"I don't know," Little Dov said. "I wish I did. I'll ask them myself as soon as I leave the hospital."

"Do you want to know what they said at the police station?"

"Yeah. Shoot."

"They said you ruined their boats," Dov said. "Ruined the engines."

"They're crazy. Why would I do anything like that?"

"Who else would? You and they are the only fishermen here. And you were squabbling constantly. Who else could have done it?"

"I don't know and I don't care," Little Dov said. "I didn't do it. You know I wouldn't lie to you."

"Were you on the beach last night?"

"I go to the beach every night," Little Dov said. "With Esther, so that you can sleep. So that you can feel at home in my house."

"Can you swear by the Ten Commandments that you didn't do it?"

"Cover my head with something and I will."

"Okay, you don't have to. I believe you. Then who did it? And why?"

"I don't know," Little Dov said. "And it's none of my business. I'm neither a snoop nor a cop. I'm a fisherman, because that's what I wanted to be and that's the trade I learned."

"But you were on the beach at night, weren't you?"

"So what? Anybody can go to the beach at night. Haven't you ever gone to the beach at night?"

"No," Dov said.

"Then you can start going now," his brother said. "And I'll stay at home with my wife, in bed. She has counted all the stars in the sky by now, and the outdoors is beginning to bore her."

"I wonder who could have done it," Dov said.

"What do you care? Are you a cop? Let the fuzz work it out. What do you care?"

"You're acting like a child," Dov said. "Things don't look good for you."

"Esther is my witness."

"I don't know if the court will accept her testimony. She's your wife."

"Look," Little Dov said, "this is beginning to bore me. Leave the guesswork to the cops and the courts. That's what they're there for. I know nothing. I don't follow anybody around. I don't go running to Israel to tell him I saw his girlfriend on the beach last night. It's none of my business."

"Who was she with?" Dov asked. "Some guy?"

"No, she was alone. When I saw her, I pulled Esther deeper into the shadows. I had no desire to talk to her and didn't want her to bother us."

"Are you sure it was her?"

"I'm bored with all this," Little Dov said. "And I feel sleepy. I guess they must have given me something."

"Okay. Do you want anything? Maybe something to read?"

"I want Esther to visit me," Little Dov said. "You know, I'm all bandaged up." He pulled back the blanket; his lower abdomen and his thighs were covered with bandages. "I feel dead down there," he said. "As if I didn't have anything. I want to see her. I know that when I touch her my body will come alive."

"All right," Dov said.

"You know," Little Dov said, turning his face to the wall, "I haven't had her for three days now. I don't know what's come over her."

"Remember Esther is a woman. Maybe she has her period."

"Esther is my wife," Little Dov said. "Her period never stopped us before."

"I'll tell her. And I'll tell her to bring you something to read."

"I don't want anything to read. I want to touch her."

"Okay, I'll tell her you want her to visit you and you want to touch her."

"And when I get back home, I'll say to her what one American soldier said to his wife when he came back from Korea. He took her to the window and said, See those trees over there? See how beautiful they are? See how beautiful the sky is? Well, have a good look, because the only thing you're going to see for the next two weeks is the ceiling. Good night, Dov."

"Good night," Dov said. "Sleep well."

He went out and began to look for the doctor, and

finally found him by the stairs, smoking a cigarette.

"Well? How is he?" the doctor said.

"That's what I expect you to tell me," Dov said. "You're the doctor."

"Dov, do you remember that the doctors declared you temporarily insane after you killed that man you found with your wife?"

"So even you know about it?"

"Dov," the doctor said, "the fact that they declared you temporarily insane was the only reason you didn't go to jail. But that can happen only once. I'm telling you this as a doctor, not as a cop."

"Why are you telling me this at all?" Dov asked. "I'm okay now. You should be worrying about my brother."

"The reason I'm telling you is so you'll know that if you do anything rash, nobody can help you. Your brother will never be a man again, Dov."

"I see," Dov said softly. "That's why he feels dead down there."

"We give him morphine, Dov," the doctor said. "And we'll keep him on sedatives for the next few days. And then we'll have to discharge him. And only then will he find out the truth."

"How did it happen?"

"One of those men was wearing spiked shoes," the doctor said. "And when he started kicking your brother he did irreversible damage to the tissue."

"You mean my brother will never—" Dov began, but he couldn't finish.

"Yes," the doctor said. "Never again."

"What about his wife?"

"After some time he'll stop caring."

"After how long?"

"I don't know," the doctor said. "Nobody knows."

"And what if he never stops caring?" Dov asked. "What if he thinks about it constantly and suffers all the time?

What then?"

"I don't know," the doctor said again. "And neither do you. Nor does he. Only God knows, but nobody can make God tell him the answer. Can you?"

"No," Dov said.

"I can't either. I did all I could so your brother wouldn't suffer. And I'll do all I can so that he'll find out the truth as late as possible. But that's all I can do. The rest is up to you. His family."

"I'd like to go now."

"You can go. Just remember what I told you. I told you that as a doctor, not a cop."

"Then, as a doctor, tell me one more thing: what will happen to those men? What will happen to them for doing what they did?"

"They'll stand trial."

"Charged with what?"

"Accidental mayhem."

"And what sentences will they get?"

"I don't know. Maybe five years each. Maybe ten."

"And then they'll come back to their women," Dov said. "To their wives, their whores, and enjoy themselves with them, doing things he'll never be able to do again as long as he lives. Isn't that so?"

"I don't think anybody can make the charge of intentional mayhem stick," the doctor said.

"If you were a real doctor," Dov said, "you'd know there's only one thing you can do for my brother. If you were a real doctor who understands people, and not just a man in a white coat."

"Shhh," the doctor said. "This is a hospital. In each of these rooms there's some poor wretch who believes we can help him. Even if you don't."

"Have they been arrested yet?"

"No," the doctor said. "The police are waiting for my report, the medical evaluation of your brother's injuries."

"When will you have it ready?"

"It's ready"

"Give it to me," Dov said. "I'll take it to the police station."

"You really will?"

"Yes," Dov said. "That sexless thing lying in that room used to be my brother."

"Maybe it's only now that he'll begin to be your brother," the doctor said. "Now that he'll need your love, your help."

"You said that," Dov said.

H E STOPPED OUTSIDE THE HOSPITAL, HOLDING THE large, sealed envelope. It was already dark. Without looking behind him, he tore the envelope into pieces and threw it away. He checked his watch; it was eight. He drove slowly through town, gazing at the dark sky, the first stars over the bay, feeling the first breeze begin to blow. He stopped the jeep in front of his brother's house, but he didn't go in. For a while he stood there, breathing hard and looking at the lighted window.

"Esther!" he called quietly.

She came out a moment later.

"Esther," he said, "bring me that picture of Dov that's hanging on the wall. And get me my leather wrist straps. You'll find them in my bag."

"Why don't you come and get them yourself?"

"Bring me everything, Esther," he said softly. "I'm tired. I never asked you for anything. But I'm asking you now."

She came back a short while later; he held out his hands and she fastened the bands around his wrists.

"What do you want to do?" she asked.

"I have to go after a few fish for my brother's sake," he said.

"And why do you need his picture?"

He took his brother's picture from her and looked at it for a moment. "You'll never be like this again," he said, and smashed it against the wall.

"What happened to him?"

"Nothing, Esther. You'll find out. With time everybody will. Now come closer."

When she did, he drew her against him and kissed her hard, making her part her lips, and felt her body cling to his, passing on its warmth—now that the day was over, had burned itself out in the sweltering heat. He felt her hands pulling his head closer and he pushed her gently away.

"I needed that," he said. "He's my brother."

"I don't care about him," she said.

He moved back a step.

"You don't care about him?"

"No," she said. "You can hit me if you want. He was right."

"Who was?"

"Israel, your friend."

"What are you talking about, Esther?"

"It wasn't that woman who was after you," she said. "It was me. I wanted you! If anything's happened, it's my fault."

"Do all you women have to be like this?" he asked. "Can't you even pretend to feel shame?"

"I speak only for myself," she said. "But no, I can't pretend to feel shame. And I can't pretend to feel love. Ask your brother."

"He loves you," he said. "And he's waiting for you."

"But I love you," she said. "And I'm waiting for you."

"Do you know, Esther, that I could have you now if I wanted? I really could?"

"You could have had me always," she said. "You could have had me the day you came to this house."

"I won't walk into this house again," Dov said. "I won't enter it until I fix those men like they fixed my brother."

"We don't have to go in," Esther said. "You can have me anyplace, anytime."

He gazed at her for a moment, then climbed into the jeep.

"Tell my father that he's old," he said. "And God will take pity on him and take him away."

"And who'll take pity on me?" Esther asked.

"Go in and wait," he said.

"Now that you're wearing those wrist straps I've nothing to wait for," Esther said.

She turned around and walked back into the house. He could still feel the warmth and smell of her body; driving down the dark side streets he thought of her firm young lips, and it was harder to bear than pain. He parked the jeep a hundred yards away from the garage and approached the low building on foot. He walked inside and looked at the man sitting in the grease pit and drinking beer. Then he looked at the man's shoes.

"Do you know what's happened?" he asked.

"Not everything's happened yet," the man said.

"Where are the others?"

"They left."

"They left or ran away?"

"They left," the man said. "You can't run away. There's nowhere to run to. I spent five years in Auschwitz; I know. But they weren't there, so they might not know."

"Why didn't you go with them?" Dov asked.

The man looked up at him. "I was waiting for you," he said.

"And what would you do in my place?"

"Same thing as you're going to do, Dov."

"Do you know he'll never be a man again?"

"I didn't want that," the man said. "That's why I stayed. I've been waiting for you for hours."

"Give me some beer," Dov said. "I'm thirsty. Throw me your bottle."

The man tossed him the bottle and Dov caught it. The beer was warm; he took a mouthful and gave the bottle back.

"Why didn't you leave with them?" he asked again.

He was already sitting in the GMC truck and driving slowly toward the man standing in the shallow pit; then he turned on the headlights, blinding him. The truck's front bumper touched the man's breast.

"If you live, we'll meet in jail," Dov Ben Dov said. "We'll be doing time for the same thing. Accidental mayhem. And then we'll come back to our women."

He closed his eyes, let in the clutch and with all his force stepped on the gas. For a moment he heard the screech of tires turning in place, and then—with his eyes still closed—he backed the truck out from over the pit, switched off the headlights, and drove out of the garage into the yard.

He walked back to the jeep and drove off fast without turning on the headlights. He parked close to the street on which his brother's house was, and, making his way through the back alley, reached the house where Ursula was staying. He peered inside through the window; she was sitting on the bed, exactly like two days ago, a book by her side. He gave the door a push and walked in.

"Are you waiting for me, too?" he asked.

"Yes," she said.

"It's strange how everybody seems to be waiting for me today," he said. "Esther, Yehuda, and now you, Ursula. All my life nobody would wait for me, and now nobody wants to run away from me. Before, everybody used to run." He held out his hand. "Come. Come with me."

"Where do you want to take me?"

"I won't harm you," he said. "I wouldn't ask you to leave this room if I wanted to hurt you. I want to talk to you, but the cops may be on my tail any moment. And they'll come here. My jeep's parked only a dozen yards away." Once again he held out his hand. "Get up and come with me," he said.

He went out and started walking toward the jeep; he knew—without turning his head—that she was following. She sat down next to him, and he began to drive along side streets and alleys, again with his lights off, heading for the desert.

"Things went wrong," he said.

"What happened to your brother?" she asked.

"I no longer have a brother," he said. "That thing in the hospital is not my brother. It's neither a man nor a woman."

"Is he dead?"

"No," he said. "He'll live. But he'll never be a man again."

"Oh my God!" she said. "That can't be true."

"It is," he said softly. "And there is nothing you can do about it. You should've thought about that earlier. Before you put sand in the engines of their boats. But you couldn't foresee this, could you? You just wanted to get me involved in my brother's feud with the fishermen so I'd get sent off to jail. Then Israel would leave with you. Was that your plan?"

"Yes," she said.

He stopped the car.

"I won't even have time to say good-bye to Israel," he said. "Take this jeep, the two of you, and leave Eilat as quickly as you can. You should be in Tel Aviv by morning. Get on the first plane and leave this country."

"And you, Dov?"

"I was born here," he said. "My father's here. And so is that thing which used to be my brother."

He climbed out of the jeep.

"Will you know how to find your way back?" he asked.

"I think so," she said. She got out of the jeep, too, and stood next to him. "Is there anything I can do?"

"No," he said. "Everything's done now."

"Why did it all have to end like this?" she asked. "You never really liked him, you know. You probably didn't even realize that, did you? You just wanted to have him next to you like a mirror, to see yourself in his eyes. But maybe you weren't aware of it."

"I see it all now," he said. "But I can't change anything. Take the jeep and leave Eilat."

"That's why he sent you over to me that night," she said. "So that he could come to me the next night and prove to himself that there's something at which he is—if not better than you—then at least your equal."

"Good-bye, Ursula," he said. "The two of you don't have much time."

"But I want you to understand," she said. "I can't just leave after what happened to your brother."

"No woman can leave after she's ruined everything," he said.

"Don't you really understand anything at all?" she asked.

"You know how to talk beautifully," he said. "Each of you, you goddamn whores, can talk better and faster than I can. I'm sure you'd love to be a man, wouldn't you?"

"Wouldn't you?" she asked.

He slapped her with all his strength; she fell backwards, hitting her head against the jeep's hood, and when she rose to her feet, he slapped her again; once again, she fell against the jeep, but this time her head struck the bumper and she didn't get up.

"I'm sorry," he said. "I didn't want that. Get up." When she didn't respond, he said again, "Get up. You don't have much time. You have to reach Tel Aviv by morning. That'll be best for everybody."

But she didn't move. He leaned over her, turning her face to the sky, then switched on the headlights. Her eyes remained open and empty.

"ISRAEL," HE CALLED OUT SOFTLY.

His friend turned in his direction. "Where are you?"

"Here," Dov said. "I've been waiting for you."

Israel walked up to him. "Ursula's not home?"

"No," Dov said. "That's why I'm waiting for you here."

"Why didn't you go in?"

"Come with me," Dov said. "You've got to help me."

He went ahead and climbed into the jeep parked in yet another spot. He drove fast, but not down back alleys as before—he drove straight along the road leading to the desert.

"You know what happened to my brother?" he asked.

"I know he's in the hospital."

"He'll be impotent for the rest of his life," Dov said. "Do you know why they did it to him?"

"No," Israel said. "I—"

Dov interrupted him. "Because Ursula ruined their boats," he said. "And I don't need to explain to you why she did that, do I?"

He stopped the jeep, turned off the headlights, and started walking. Israel followed him. Finally Dov came to a standstill and waited for Israel to catch up with him.

"Over there," Dov said.

"What's that?" Israel asked.

"That's her," Dov said.

Israel walked up to him slowly. "What happened to her?"

"She's dead."

"You killed her?"

"No," Dov said. "She insulted me, so I slapped her in

136

the face. She fell, hit her head against the bumper, and didn't get up."

Israel stepped back. "What will you do?"

"I'll do what I have to do," Dov said. "I'll go to the police and tell them what happened."

"Then go," Israel said. "Why did you bring me here?"

"To tell you how it happened," Dov said.

"Tell that to the police."

"I want you to be my witness," Dov said. "Don't turn away."

"I can't be your witness," Israel said. "I wasn't here with you."

"That's why I brought you here. To tell you how it happened."

Israel looked at him. "Do you really think any judge would believe me? Don't you remember how it was the last time, when I said I started the fight? Nobody believed me. Why should anybody believe me now?" He walked over to Ursula's body and knelt down by it. "Get up," he said. "Stop this game and get up, damn you!" He began throwing handfuls of sand in her face. "Get up!"

"She won't," Dov said. "She's dead."

Israel lifted his gaze to him. "Why should I testify? I wasn't here. Nobody was. And even if I was, I would've turned my back. I can't bear to look at such things. Why me?"

"Because I have only you," Dov said.

"Listen," Israel said, still kneeling by Ursula's body, "I can't. I'm a weak man. Nobody's going to believe me. And why should they? You've killed before."

"Israel," Dov said softly, "you'll have to do what I'm asking."

"And what if they won't believe me? If they sentence us both?"

"They won't sentence you," Dov said. "They'll only sentence me." He took a step toward Israel. "But even if they put us both behind bars, didn't you tell me yesterday you'd always stick with me? Didn't you say that? And it's your woman's fault that my brother has become a eunuch!"

"I can't do it, Dov," Israel said. "The police will think we did it together."

"And we did," Dov said.

"I wasn't here," Israel said.

"But you were there when you told me I should go to her," Dov said. "And that's when she began to hate me and I began to hate her." He placed his hand on Israel's arm. "Can't you understand that only you can help me now?"

"No," Israel said. "I can't help you. I wasn't here. I know how it'll be; they'll start asking me questions, more and more questions, and they'll shine a lamp in my face until I finally tell them whatever they want to hear. I know I'll tell them. I'm a weak man, that's all."

"Look, you simply have to help me," Dov said. "Like I've always helped you."

"Yes," Israel said. "You always helped me." Suddenly he put his face against Ursula's breast. "Dov," he said, "she's alive. She's breathing."

He got up; Dov knelt next to Ursula's body and placed his head on her breast. Israel held the stone ready in his hand; he had noticed it while kneeling by Ursula's body, and he picked it up while pressing his face to her chest. He waited until he saw Dov begin to straighten up, then he hit him twice in quick succession; he circled the body to make sure Dov was really dead, then hit him a third time; only then did he toss the stone away.

THEY LEFT THE BAY BEHIND. IN FRONT OF THEM WAS open desert. He was uncomfortable; his hands were handcuffed, and he could barely move them.

"Take these off," he said. "You know I won't run away."

"Should I take them off?" one of the cops asked.

"No," the other cop said. "Rules are rules." He turned to Israel. "You can stand it, man. This whole thing will surely resolve itself in the next few days. You have nothing to fear if you were trying to defend that woman like you say."

They were driving past the hospital. Suddenly Israel saw Esther.

"Stop for a moment, okay?" he said to the cops. "I want to say goodbye to her."

They pulled up to the curb.

"Let me know if I can help you in any way," he said.

"We don't need your help," she said.

"Remember our conversation? Do you now know what I was talking about?" he asked her softly.

"I don't care what you were talking about," she said. "I'm going to have a child, you know." She looked at him for a moment. "I've never loved anybody but Dov," she said. "And I'll go on loving him for the rest of my life."

"I know," Israel said. "I always knew you loved Dov." He turned to the cops. "We can drive on."

She gazed after them, her hands folded across her belly, then she turned around. She looked at the wide open hospital door through which—his arms spread wide to embrace her—Little Dov was coming out.

Madrid, June 1963

139

Guys Like Me by Dominique Fabre

Dominique Fabre, born in Paris and a life-long resident of the city, exposes the shadowy, anonymous lives of many who inhabit the French capital. In this quiet, subdued tale, a middle-aged office worker, divorced and alienated from his only son, meets up with two childhood friends who are similarly adrift. He's looking for a second act to his mournful life, seeking the harbor of love and a true connection with his son. Set in palpably real Paris streets that feel miles away from the City of Light, a stirring novel of regret and absence, yet not without a glimmer of hope.

I Called Him Necktie by Milena Michiko Flašar

Twenty-year-old Taguchi Hiro has spent the last two years of his life living as a hikikomori—a shut-in who never leaves his room and has no human interaction—in his parents' home in Tokyo. As Hiro tentatively decides to reenter the world, he spends his days observing life from a park bench. Gradually he makes friends with Ohara Tetsu, a salaryman who has lost his job. The two discover in their sadness a common bond. This beautiful novel is moving, unforgettable, and full of surprises.

Who is Martha? by Marjana Gaponenko

In this rollicking novel, 96-year-old ornithologist Luka Levadski foregoes treatment for lung cancer and moves from Ukraine to Vienna to make a grand exit in a luxury suite at the Hotel Imperial. He reflects on his past while indulging in Viennese cakes and savoring music in a gilded concert hall. Levadski was born in 1914, the same year that Martha—the last of the now-extinct passenger pigeons—died. Levadski himself has an acute sense of being the last of a species. This gloriously written tale mixes piquant wit with lofty musings about life, friendship, aging and death.

KILLING AUNTIE BY ANDRZEJ BURSA

A university student named Jurek finds himself with nothing to do. After his doting aunt asks the young man to perform a small chore, he decides to kill her for no good reason. This short comedic masterpiece combines elements of Dostoevsky, Sartre, Kafka and Heller to produce an unforgettable tale of murder and—just maybe—redemption.

ALEXANDRIAN SUMMER BY YITZHAK GORMEZANO GOREN

This is the story of two Jewish families living their frenzied last days in the doomed cosmopolitan social whirl of Alexandria just before fleeing Egypt for Israel in 1951. The conventions of the Egyptian upper-middle class are laid bare in this dazzling novel, which exposes sexual hypocrisies and portrays a vanished polyglot world of horse-racing, seaside promenades and nightclubs.

COCAINE BY PITIGRILLI

Paris in the 1920s—dizzy and decadent. Where a young man can make a fortune with his wits ... unless he is led into temptation. Cocaine's dandified hero Tito Arnaudi invents lurid scandals and gruesome deaths, and sells these stories to the newspapers. But his own life becomes even more outrageous when he acquires three demanding mistresses. Elegant, witty and wicked, Pitigrilli's classic novel was first published in Italian in 1921 and retains its venom even today.

SOME DAY BY SHEMI ZARHIN

On the shores of Israel's Sea of Galilee lies the city of Tiberias, a place bursting with sexuality and longing for love. The air is saturated with smells of cooking and passion. Some Day is a gripping family saga, a sensual and emotional feast that plays out over decades. This is an enchanting tale about tragic fates that disrupt families and break our hearts. Zarhin's hypnotic writing renders a painfully delicious vision of individual lives behind Israel's larger national story.

THE MISSING YEAR OF JUAN SALVATIERRA BY PEDRO MAIRAL

At the age of nine, Juan Salvatierra became mute following a horse riding accident. At twenty, he began secretly painting a series of canvases on which he detailed six decades of life in his village on Argentina's frontier with Uruguay. After his death, his sons return to deal with their inheritance: a shed packed with rolls over two miles long. But an essential roll is missing. A search ensues that illuminates links between art and life, with past family secrets casting their shadows on the present.

THE GOOD LIFE ELSEWHERE BY VLADIMIR LORCHENKOV

The very funny—and very sad—story of a group of villagers and their tragicomic efforts to emigrate from Europe's most impoverished nation to Italy for work. An Orthodox priest is deserted by his wife for an art-dealing atheist; a mechanic redesigns his tractor for travel by air and sea; and thousands of villagers take to the road on a modern-day religious crusade to make it to the Italian Promised Land. A country where 25 percent of its population works abroad, remittances make up nearly 40 percent of GDP, and alcohol consumption per capita is the world's highest – Moldova surely has its problems. But, as Lorchenkov vividly shows, it's also a country whose residents don't give up easily.

KILLING THE SECOND DOG BY MAREK HLASKO

Two down-and-out Polish con men living in Israel in the 1950s scam an American widow visiting the country. Robert, who masterminds the scheme, and Jacob, who acts it out, are tough, desperate men, exiled from their native land and adrift in the hot, nasty underworld of Tel Aviv. Robert arranges for Jacob to run into the widow who has enough trouble with her young son to keep her occupied all day. What follows is a story of romance, deception, cruelty and shame. Hlasko's writing combines brutal realism with smoky, hardboiled dialogue, in a bleak world where violence is the norm and love is often only an act.

FANNY VON ARNSTEIN: DAUGHTER OF THE ENLIGHTENMENT BY HILDE SPIEL

In 1776 Fanny von Arnstein, the daughter of the Jewish master of the royal mint in Berlin, came to Vienna as an 18-year-old bride. She married a financier to the Austro-Hungarian imperial court, and hosted an ever more splendid salon which attracted luminaries of the day. Spiel's elegantly written and carefully researched biography provides a vivid portrait of a passionate woman who advocated for the rights of Jews, and illuminates a central era in European cultural and social history.

New Vessel Press

To purchase these titles and for more information please visit
newvesselpress.com.